Bodies
in
Motion

Zane (Hickcox) Kotker

Middlebury '56

Bodies
in
Motion

by Zane Kotker

NEW YORK
ALFRED A. KNOPF

 1972

This is a Borzoi Book
Published by Alfred A. Knopf, Inc.

Copyright © 1972 by Zane Kotker
All rights reserved under International and Pan-American Copyright Conventions. Published in the United States by Alfred A. Knopf, Inc., New York, and simultaneously in Canada by Random House of Canada Limited, Toronto. Distributed by Random House, Inc., New York.

Library of Congress Cataloging in Publication Data
Kotker, Zane. Bodies in motion.
I. Title.
PZ4.K869Bo [PS3561.0845] 813'.5'4 76-181368
ISBN 0-394-47891-6

Manufactured in the United States of America

FIRST EDITION

To Norman, in the pair bond

Contents

Bodies
in
Motion

Earthward

Strands of exposed film hung from Sonya's shower rail and blew gently in the draft circulating above the tub. The window to the airshaft was stuck open and soot always coated the bottles of developing chemicals that stood on the tile shelf. Sonya wondered how much soot was floating over the empty tub and getting caught on the delicate layers of silver she had that morning indelibly etched in slightly varying shades of gray. The smell of developing chemicals was beginning to fade from the stuffy bathroom but for months now it had never entirely vanished; Sonya accepted its permanent presence as the price the old folks in heaven would dock her for a brilliant terrific wow career as a photographer of note.

3

At the height of summer she had gotten up before dawn on a Sunday morning to check lighting conditions from the promenade near the 79th Street Boat Basin where she was executing an intricate series of shots of the water surface from different angles. She tried to imprint on the gummy paper the pull and tension on the surface of the water—the ridges, like mountains, that were thrown up as minute waves on a square yard of Hudson's oily waters. Sonya enjoyed the slow examination of things from unfamiliar points of view. What had happened to Alice in Wonderland had not been denied Sonya in Oregon. When distortions of natural phenomena were not forthcoming Sonya herself would narrow her eyelids to a slit or stare outward until her eyes grew dry in order to see ordinary things afresh.

All this took time and solitude and Sonya had plenty of each. Her phone had scarcely rung during the weekends she had devoted to right angles. She had warmed up for that exercise by staring at the corners of her furniture and at the exact points where her walls changed direction, where pieces of paper became eastbound instead of north, and where tubs went on their private journeys. Then she began to photograph these mysterious happenings in all their blustering precision. Although Sonya could not, her friends took right angles for granted and avoided her when she announced the onset of such a project. So Sonya went on ahead, leaving her friends to chuckle as she forged her way through the universe splitting the air before her with

4

a secret ray in the manner of comic book heroines wearing brass circles on their breasts. Or so she liked to think.

Alone, immersed in air, buffeted by waves of light, sound, and heat, Sonya marched forward with a metal box held before her right eye, leaving behind her a trail of celluloid strips like hundreds of delicate tails. Back and forth she plodded, over the floorboards of the two-bedroom apartment she had inherited the preceding year from a maiden aunt. The ring her coffee cup made in the morning on the sill in the bedroom-become-dark-room was still discernible, dried, at evening and the central hallway, where traffic had been thickest, seemed to echo to her sensitive ears with the snapping of molecules that moved back into place after her passage. Sonya among the elements, such was her life until the fall when she met Victor.

Victor was big and bearlike with a barrel chest and curly hair; he sweated a lot as he propelled himself emphatically about. He preserved the mannerisms acquired on a summer job in Roxbury. Collecting back bills, he had skulked around neighborhood bars in a trenchcoat listening for the whereabouts of a vulnerable Pearl or Vivia and only somewhat guiltily reveling in the glorious spy charade. Now, after a bit of law school, a few years in Europe, and a stint on an upstate newspaper, he was assigned to the news desk of a television network. And, although he didn't go out on camera, he nevertheless enjoyed cupping his hand to light a cigarette in Sonya's fourth-floor apartment or casting a practiced glance over his shoulder at the door that was overprotected with two Segal locks. Sonya loved it all and when she laid her hand on Victor's neck where the fuzzy hair ran to flesh she was happy, indeed, captivated; her sensitivity to environment was shattered, leaving her oblivious to anything but Victor. They married.

Victor moved in, bringing his skis and ski boots, his bicycle, his father's one-volume Dante, and his brother's serial Christmas gifts—the complete back issues of the Life World Library, from the Andean Republics to Yugoslavia. There was his walnut table made from a door, his oak couch made from a second door, his brass spool bed transported from a New Hampshire uncle's barn, and, from a Brooklyn outlet, five or six wicker statues that looked like Easter Island heads. These bulky giants filled up the empty spaces around Aunt Monica's spindly French tables and her spidery carved music stand.

Sonya allowed Victor to place his ski stuff temporarily in her darkroom. Gingerly the boy spy leaned his Harts against the enlarger and placed his boots on the print dryer. After all, the apartment had been hers, it was at her generosity that Victor had been invited at all, or so he reasoned in the shy way of brides and grooms who must suddenly inhabit legally the apartments of their lovers, with all their revealing, even embarrassing belongings. Sonya, for her part, worried at the great relief she felt when Victor's skis were finally lifted and moved to the freshly cleaned bedroom closet. She had not developed a single negative during the week that the skis had rested on her equipment. But then, she was newlywed, she kept telling herself. There was no significance to it. And so the two who had been grandly living life as separate centers of universes bid farewell to their adolescences and set up together as a pair. After a decent interval, Sonya went back to working an occasional evening in the darkroom while Victor's pupils widened over the pages of far-off *France* and *The Two Chinas.*

Victor wanted Sonya to be a photographer; if he, Victor, were not an ordinary man, why should he tie up with an ordinary woman? So he took his wife out to eat a lot and encouraged her to use frozen (gourmet) foods. On those days when Sonya rushed home from her job with the diaper company—an interim post between her past on the Portland paper and her future among the greats, a job where she daily photographed twenty babies atop their mothers' dining tables without once mouthing the indoctrination gambit, "If you don't buy anything, we throw out your baby's proofs"—and hurried into the darkroom to finish her portfolio, Victor would press onward into *Russia* and *Japan.* But eventually he tired of examining foreign, Ektachrome territories and turned homeward to his own future. Landless, anonymous, a man like other men. Maybe he could still slip out of the whirring electronic team of television and go back to the wilds? Maybe he could manage somebody else's ski resort or, better, build one of his own? Always before, he had fallen back on the possibility of ski bumming at Vail, but that was out of the question now; he was married.

"Snow, Sonya, beautiful white snow. You could shoot it all year round." Victor swung his legs onto Aunt Monica's newly scarred coffee table and spit cherry pits into the wastebasket.

"Trees, Sonya, thin leafless little trees lifting themselves up in the snow. You can do it, Sonya baby, you can survive the wilds with me." He placed the wastebasket between his thighs.

"But of course," Sonya replied, pulling a new print around the table edge to break the paper so it wouldn't curl, her flat, wide fingertips sticking to the paper in the heat of their first summer. "Whither thou goest, I will go." But would she? Now that she had followed her maiden aunt to New York, through years of family photograph albums, could she give up the anonymous faces, the marvelous clutter, the pride in having lifted off from *Our Town* and soared away from the physical landscape of Oregon to the human landscape of the city? It was this journey, paradoxically, and this new environment that had freed her to take her camera back to the physical world, the currents of air, the breeze disturbing the dust, and the sunlight on windowsills that had become her special kingdom. Thrown back onto a physical landscape, she would have nothing to report, she'd simply be living it.

"Why, Victor," she put down the print and pushed her light brown hair behind her ears. "Let me wash more cherries for you."

Victor decided on an extreme measure. He'd save all their money to buy skiing land, a whole mountain. Mountains, in fact, a chain of mountains, chains of mountains, the Himalayas, the entire East! Throw in Peking and she'd come; it was, reportedly, urban. Worth a chance.

"Don't throw out the half-rotten cherries," he called into the kitchen. "Cut off the good part, we're going on a budget."

After that, Victor gave up the World Library and spent his spare time on the phone trying to talk his friends into buying shares in the ski area of his dreams. Sonya finished her portfolio and landed a job as a photographer for a textbook publisher. At last she had managed to turn work into play and play into work. At her new office she was assigned to Science and every day when she checked into the studio the back of her hand was stamped in luminescent ink with the letters *Sci*. They were invisible at her office desk but they glowed the instant she opened the door into the darkroom. Other hands working in the dark beside her glowed *Soc. Stud.* and *Lang. Arts* as they hovered over the pans of chemicals. Sonya's letters seemed to glow brightest whenever she reached into the cupboard to borrow a roll of company film for herself. Victor's budget had cut her down to a solitary roll per week.

She worked at the new job for a few months, shooting protozoa through a microscope, and got pregnant.

"Maybe we can put him in the darkroom, with the shade up, of course," Victor offered as they sat on the couch, all three of them, Victor, his wife, and the unborn son he'd so recently acquired. He put his arm around them.

"Victor! I couldn't!" She was silent, stricken.

"The suburbs?" he asked, stroking her hand. His woman. His son. He could leave them secure in a house with a yard and join the other men on the train every morning. So what if other guys did it; they had their reasons.

"Okay, he can have the darkroom! I'll ask Harold if I can use the one at the office." She felt her choices narrowing, abruptly. She rose from the couch to fix a warm milk.

"And we could save money, on formula, for the ski area if you nurse, Sonya," Victor said in her direction as she left. But she didn't laugh. Was she already irritable from being pregnant? Didn't she know the suburbs would be a last resort? And that if she nursed he'd be jealous? But he'd make do? He sipped a Scotch and reopened his ski magazine. Terrific, they'd be crowded out of the apartment by babies at the exact moment when he'd gotten together the money for the ski area. In the deck house they'd have next to the lodge, he'd build Sonya an entire photographic wing. Victor turned to the monthly pull-out: a yellow-suited Norwegian in full schuss. So, it was decided. They would stay here until they had two babies, and by that time he should have the money to get out, free. It felt pleasant being put into the control of forces beyond himself. All he had to do was pedal. But would Sonya leave Sootville for the love of Victor? For a darkroom? Or maybe for the baby's lungs? Why doesn't she see the dog turds in the street? She sees everything else—a whole week on corners!

When she was about six months pregnant, Sonya went to look at the playground, or baby park, as her mother had always termed them, near the foot of her street; she was to complete a photographic assignment for the children's text, in the section on gravity. It was a January day with snow melting in blotches under the jungle gym near the entrance to the playground. Sonya went directly across the asphalt to four orange seesaws and pushed them down in the same direction. Then she circled around the slanted boards trying to catch the sun slipping down the four identical angles and find the exact location from which the boards would look drawn, pulled toward the earth. Well, not the earth exactly, but the pavement laid over the dirt piled onto cement blocks in the roof above the railroad tracks that ran far below the park. She had plenty of time to circle the scene in a semi-crouch with her camera up to her eye because there were few children in the park and none of them fancied the seesaws.

When she had satisfied herself with that, she tried balancing a single board on its metal fulcrum and shooting as it started toward the ground in one direction or the other, but she couldn't handle her camera fast enough to shoot before the board touched ground. While she was trying it the fourth time, two nurses came over to sit on the boards and warm themselves in the sun. Sonya saw the swings were free and walked toward them. While she walked, she tried to feel the attraction of the earth working on the soles of her feet but couldn't. She knew enough to know she didn't understand what the text had said about the pull of two bodies toward one another, the one with the greater mass winning the tug of war.

She let two swings hang perpendicularly down and swung the third, photographing its gradually decreasing arc until it came to rest as close to the earth as its chains allowed and finally hung without moving. The sun was warming up the park and more children were arriving. She hurried to the metal slide, walked around the side of it and looked into the sun so that the whole

slope of the slide—an abstract hillside—was silhouetted against the sun, except for a narrow band where
the sun glinted down its length. She barely had time
to shoot before a boy wearing a Superman cape hurled
himself up the steps of the slide. The art director had
said: "No children in any of the pictures, just objects
demonstrating gravity. We'll put the children in later."

There were boys and girls perched at various levels
of the jungle gym and Sonya realized the park was
getting inconveniently overpopulated. She placed the
rubber-bound camera strap over her shoulder and
stuffed her cold fingers into her pockets. She noticed
the children's feet as they jumped and slid and ran in
the park, imagining comic book rays of power ema-
nating from the earth, holding the creatures to it
through the soles of their feet. She didn't understand
gravity at all.

She walked out of the playground to the surrounding park. The voices of the children faded as she walked
south over rocks in which iron particles were lined up
north-south pointing to a single location on the great
mass of the earth which pulled her close and was in
turn pulled close and kept in orbit by the sun's mass.
She stepped to one side of the trickle of melting snow
that ran down the paved slope she was climbing. Why
does water run downhill? The bottom of the hill is closer
to the inner mass of the earth than the top. She had
never thought of *that* before!

She crouched at the bottom of the hill and focused

her camera on the bright, sun-reflecting flow of water that slid thinly over the pavement covering the small hillside. The air was clear, her breath fogged the eyepiece of the camera. Everything was very bright, objects seemed to be outlined with thin black lines as in the work of precise German photographers. Her assignment was completed. She should stay on and photograph something falling through the air, but the leaves had left the trees long ago and there was no forecast of snow. She felt tired and she started home.

She quit work in March with the option to take on free-lance assignments after the baby was born. Gravity left her mind until the birth of the child, when, lying on the labor table, she had a vision of the baby's head being pulled out of her toward the ground by the pull of the planet but this belied the contractions of her own muscles. The milk ran from her nipples toward the ground and she feared dropping the baby when she first picked it up. The flowers friends sent her wilted and drooped over the edges of their vases and curtains hung around her while she rested, horizontal on her bed, a raised platform of earth.

Sonya laid her infant son in a giant carriage with polished handlebars that reflected the sun handsomely and contentedly wheeled him in the quieter areas of the park that had been planted by the Hudson. In June

Peter could raise his head and push his torso up by pressing his arms and hands against the carriage mattress. During the summer, Sonya set him on a blanket atop the grass while she read or polished her nails and he taught himself to roll over. By September he sat up, his muscles developing their control slowly, downward from his head and neck through his back and hips until they could support the column of his trunk and he could sit without crumpling. As snow fell they sat side by side on a cold bench by the river, watching boats and eating bananas. Peter raised his arms to Sonya and she held him up on his feet where he laughed out loud as his knees locked and he balanced precariously. As the year edged out of Peter's first winter, his love of feeling pressure against the bottom of his feet became a passion, and he stood alone by holding onto a bench on the esplanade until one day he let go and took a few steps to the side, and walked. With these steps he ceased to be a creature of the wilds, the glens and shadowy places of Riverside Park, its open esplanade, its river wall, its pile of rock; he was taken into the baby park to become a social being.

The Chinese Dancers

Two adult humans lay in the area, side by side; the child lay a short distance away. Sleep still held the bodies horizontal, body temperatures rested at their coolest point of the night. About four A.M. the bodies began to warm, gradually regaining the three degrees of temperature lost during the night. Blood pressure swelled against the walls of the arteries and the adrenal glands sent hormones flowing into the bloodstream. The heart's pumping lost a slow regularity and the lungs also quickened to a less predictable expansion and contraction. Images sparked the synapses of the brain, eyeballs followed the moving images. There were beasts to watch, predators, the chase, sudden pouncings. The terror of life during the predawn hours, when stalking was at its peak, flitted from synapse to synapse in the sleeping brains.

The baby cried. The sound no longer caused milk to run from Sonya's nipples but it still woke her instantly. Peter would be standing in his crib, holding out his arms to her, his uncut hair curling at the nape of his neck. Having a child had been, at the beginning, like a love affair. Sonya had been saddened when the baby slept, impatient for his naps to end. Her completion, a sense of being at rest, not urgently pushed by time, came when she was holding Peter. But a year after his birth and she often tensed at Peter's morning cry, wanting to sleep a little longer herself, or to be with Victor, lying along the warmth of his body beneath the sheet.

She sat up and leaned over Victor, who slept with the sheet wrapping him into a huge cocoon of white that nevertheless appeared to encase life since it moved up and down with breathing, gave off warmth, and smelled human, even masculine. She pressed her forehead against his sheeted neck, he smelled like men, like Victor. The baby's cries increased. She breathed in Victor's smell, got up, and crossed the hallway, walking with one hip out to avoid the playpen, and entered the baby's room to pick him up. She held him close, her forearm fitting under his buttocks, his weight resting against her hip, his shoulder pressing against her breast. She walked into the kitchen, which was full of roundness; pan bottoms, juice-can tops, the can opener

—a maker of circles. She moved carefully, slowly. She chatted with her son and prepared a boiled egg for him. She had longed for a son. Boys were important. God had once been one, according to Victor's bedtime stories and other reliable sources.

Lying in bed, Victor smelled the bacon cooking, gradually began to hear Sonya's voice as she talked to the baby about circles. His own mother's conversation had been limited to household and family events. He unwrapped his head from the sheet; he could lie in the sunlight, which sucked blue from the curtains, tinging the whole bed blue, for another hour or more. He wasn't expected in the newsroom until ten forty-five, but it was lonely in bed. He heard the bacon begin to sizzle. Sonya the passionate, frying bacon! A woman whose bemused and wistful exterior had promised never to turn into that of the methodical housewife; a woman to whom a chair was not an object to be dusted but only considered! What had he done to her? A Wasp gone *Mammamia* so soon? Had his Italian genes corrupted her?

"Sonya!" He sat up in bed, guiltily. He would apologize. "Hey! Sonya!" but she didn't come. She was with the baby.

"In Italy, women tend to the man first!" He called desperately, knowing it wasn't true but grasping at anything that might bring her to his bedside.

"I'm changing the baby," she called back from his son's room. To a practiced ear, she sounded the slightest bit annoyed. Maybe he should simply get up. Of course, action.

Victor stood up and headed for the bathroom, catching a glimpse of Sonya's slim thighs in tight-fitting slacks. He remembered the smoothness of her thighs, but wasn't that almost a week ago? He turned the faucet on a little way, soaped his face and picked up his razor. Perhaps the only way to keep Sonya in bed in the morning was to get rich. Then they could go on vacation with a nurse, maybe even in separate planes. He turned on the faucet harder. The water pressure was minuscule. In the mountains, even in the suburbs, they probably had decent water pressure. How did that separate planes stuff work? Oh yes, Sonya'd go on one plane and he'd go on the other. No, that wasn't what he wanted. He turned the faucet on harder. What plane did the nurse go on? And would she be a red-cheeked Irish girl? The faucet slipped past the point where it ordinarily stopped and still only a trickle of water fell into the bowl. He kept turning, on and on, imagining a fleet of planes in V-formation carrying the famous TV analyst, his family, and entourage all dressed in fun furs from winter spa to winter spa. He saw them in the morning taking early runs through Swiss fields: himself, Sonya, the little fellow, the nurse.

The light above the medicine chest had gone out. Glass was falling on his hand. He was holding a detached faucet handle in his left hand. Joseph & Mary. A torrent of water was shooting out of the headless water spigot, straight up into the air, cresting at forehead level and slopping onto the floor. He felt the water on the soles of his feet.

"Sonya!" he shouted.

"What's the matter?" she called.

"Oh, nothing," he called back, having assessed the situation. "Just a little water in the bathroom."

"Hey!" she said, leaning over the threshold, "are you okay, Dr. Livingstone?"

"I've analyzed our water pressure problem," he answered. "We used to have too little," he explained quietly. "Now," he added, resuming his shave, "we have too much." He smiled from the drizzle.

"Spectacular!" she answered. "But what'll we do now?" She heard Peter trying to climb out of the highchair and she ran into the kitchen without staying for Victor's answer.

"Get the super!" he shouted after her.

"Sometimes it takes two weeks," she shouted back.

"Maybe you'd better start right away," he replied, working hurriedly, the mirror too steamed to show much but a hazy outline of his face.

"Plumbing is the ma-an's thing, isn't it?" she answered in a simpering Southern accent. So she was mad at his crack about Italian women. That comparison always made her feel flat-chested.

"The man takes the baby." He answered deliberately as he removed another swatch of beard. "The woman attends to household problems."

"You're sure, now?" she responded, holding the baby under one arm, throwing towels on the bathroom floor with her free hand. "We don't want to make any basic mistakes," she whispered over the water.

"Hand me the baby!" He put down the razor and she passed the baby to him and ran out the door wearing only a sweater against the March wind.

In the bedroom, Victor lifted his son to the mantelpiece. His son! "See the flowers!" he said, and Peter looked, his muscles holding up his head as if they had always been able to and his hands reaching for the paper flowers, the thumb working in opposition like a veteran, picking one slender stem from the vase without disturbing the others. The baby looked exactly like his father. The Italian features of Victor's mother were blended with the Irish coloring of his father, the old Boston success story. Victor nuzzled the baby's stomach and the boy screeched with laughter. What a terrific baby!

Sonya came back with the super in tow. Victor finished dressing.

"Getting it all fixed up in there?" Victor boomed at the super as he strode through the hallway with the baby on his arm. Mechanical things, even the teletype machines that clattered around him in the newsroom, were a mystery. He put his arm around Sonya as she slipped out of the bathroom to bid him farewell, but the baby wanted to be in the circle too, so they stood together in a huddle.

"Who are you lunching with today?" Sonya asked, suddenly feeling out of touch with Victor's daily life.

"Sandwiches. Jake's taking Samson and me on location. And what are you doing with *him* today?" Victor responded, indicating the baby and using the unidentified *he,* an understood declension of familiarity located beyond the ablative.

"We're going into the playground," she replied. "It's time he saw some other children." The two adults kissed, only their lips touching.

An hour later, Sonya walked into the playground to be publicly numbered among the professional mothers. She wanted to get settled quickly and chose the swings. She inserted Peter into a metal-barred seat and pushed it. He swung. He smiled. Sonya remembered an article from the *Times* in which it was reported that babies smile when swinging because their lowest vertebra bends pleasantly as if the lost tail were holding on to a branch. She noticed the tightness of his grasp on the metal bar, and studied his gaze as he watched the space narrowing between him and the jungle gym and then widening as he swung back. She squeezed the back of his snowsuited knees and gave him another push.

She looked at the population spread out around her on the benches that formed a circle with an opening, like a horseshoe's, near the gate. Where should she sit?

Black nursemaids sat at both ends of the horseshoe, near the gate. A few white mothers came next. Sonya's eye was drawn to the cluster of population at the apex of the horseshoe, the center of activity. Women were gathered around a sunken sandbox. But Peter was too young for that, he would only eat the sand; she lifted him from the swing and carried him to the center of the asphalt where she could stand, uncommitted, while her son played at her feet. She watched the sunken pit—a strangely compelling attraction, like the well in a photograph of her mother-in-law's dusty Sicilian birthplace. Or like the clothes-washing stream of jungle women.

Made clumsy by snowsuits, children staggered happily about in the pit, tossing sand at each other's eyes. Suddenly, two women, one pregnant, jumped up and ran to two screaming children in the pit. Sonya heard the screams subside, watched as the women returned to their bench. There, both mothers resettled and resumed the conversation. Shouts of "Mine!" "Mine!" came out of the pit at steady intervals accompanied by sounds of clashing metal or the soft whack of plastic. Again the two women jumped from their seats to the fray and resettled to their pleasant chat; from time to time their voices rose and joined others in what seemed to be a continuous shouted message— "That is not your pail, that is Paul's pail; that is not your shovel, that is Amy's shovel; that is *not* your truck, give it back; *we don't throw sand;* WE DON'T BITE!"

Sonya loosened her scarf under the noontime sun

and, picking up Peter, returned to a vacant bench behind the swings to sit and watch. Neither she nor Peter was ready for the big time—the forum where culture and civilization were imposed on last year's crop of babies, where the concepts of property and war evolved anew each forenoon. She and Peter would remain apart, along with the fetuses, warmly within their mothers' bodies, who were too young to learn, and the three-year-olds, hanging gracefully from bars, who appeared to have graduated. Sonya opened her copy of the *Times* and, maintaining her privacy, bent her head to read while watching Peter from the corner of her eye. Not until the first warm morning, when the children escaped their snowsuits and were stuffed into their heaviest sweaters, would Sonya allow herself to be drawn into fellowship.

She arrived early that morning and, with ten or so others, was treated to the sight of a woman and a man moving slowly to the inward countings of the Chinese exercise T'ai-chi-chuan. The man was middle-aged, Oriental; he was the teacher. The woman was young, with long yellow hair, bellbottom pants, and the self-conscious body movements of an actress. They wore sabers at their waists, pretentious weapons that looked as if they had been rented or stolen from a theater costume shop. The man raised an arm and then a leg in counterpose, carving a little statue in the air showing where he had been standing and occupying space before he had moved to a new location slightly to the right. The woman copied him, lagging just a fraction behind, her lips moving soundlessly as she counted, her eyes not turned toward the man at her side, but obviously viewing him peripherally, checking on which movements came next and whether the two were in accord.

At first the children did not play but joined their mothers in a silent circle of the curious around the dancing pair until the crowd doubled and tripled, thus providing a fringe where concentration lessened; here voices began to be heard, shoes to be scraped noisily. It was from here that the day at the park moved hesitantly into familiar channels. A boy in a red sweater slid down the slide in a blur and legs pumped on the swings. Within ten minutes' time, the children had left the odd dancers, but the mothers remained collected around the pair.

"Some kind of Chinese dance, I think," a woman with loose brown hair remarked to a sub-circle of like-haired mothers.

"I wouldn't want to do that in front of these people," a short woman with teased hair whispered to another with curlers. The one with curlers snickered.

The black women smiled at one another, keeping their lips closed.

The couple continued to dance, the man raising a

leg and slapping a thigh. From close up the performers had the same disappointing quality of smallness that stage performers have from the first row.

When the loose-haired women finally broke and moved off to their part of the park nearest the swings in the curve of the horseshoe, Sonya followed them. Several of them sat together on a bench. From this position the dancing couple near the now foreshortened hopscotch pattern looked larger as they moved noiselessly on the concrete, side by side, eyes straight ahead, silent, sunlit.

"She's bad in the legs, but her arm movements are okay," said a loose-haired blonde in her early twenties. She spoke in Sonya's direction, across the prominent breasts of a pucci-scarfed woman.

"Watch his shoulders now, this part coming up," the blonde said to Sonya as she handed a box of raisins to a straw-haired girl in a stroller. The girl struggled to open the raisins.

"See that? How he moved his shoulder? That's upper class. Like a wave passing up his elbow through his shoulder to his head. Very upper class. A peasant would just jerk his head, like this." The blonde demonstrated with an abrupt snap of the head.

"Can you do it?" Sonya asked as she watched Peter walking unsteadily after a ball.

"I studied a year. I only learned about seven minutes of it. It lasts twenty minutes." She laughed. The straw-haired girl screamed with frustration, unable to open the box of raisins. The blonde opened the small box for her, her long, clean hair falling across her pocketbook.

"How come you were learning it?" Sonya nudged the ball toward Peter.

"I was a dancer, that is, what the trade calls a general mover. I took T'ai-chi-chuan to keep in shape. The lessons lasted an hour and I felt great at the end, every muscle gets used." The straw-haired girl reached into the raisin box and extracted one raisin, slowly, between the index finger and the thumb. The raisin dropped.

"I've seen pictures of it in history books, I think. Lots of fellows moving their arms in the woods at dawn." Sonya stopped the ball with her foot. "But I didn't know the Communists did it," she added.

"Without it the Chinese wouldn't be Chinese. Like Finns without the sauna, Jews without the book. It's their history. It makes them Chinese." The blonde picked up the fallen raisin and tossed it over her shoulder; her daughter was cautiously extracting another raisin, which she then slowly elevated to her lips.

"How can it take a year to learn a dance?" Sonya asked.

The straw-haired girl dropped the raisin box. The blonde picked it up. "Look at it carefully! You have to practice to make those movements flow into each other. Each hand, each foot, each leg, each arm, everything has its position every second, and you have to remember when everything happens. Like learning to ride a bicycle." The blonde handed the box to the girl. The girl flung it to the pavement. "Alexandra!" the blonde scolded, bending for the box.

"I wouldn't have the patience," Sonya replied.

"Months, it takes months," the blonde continued, pouring a few raisins into her daughter's hand. "And it costs an arm and a leg," she gestured toward Alexandra. "We couldn't afford it any more."

While Alexandra pressed the palm containing the raisins to her mouth, Sonya gazed across the playground past the children running and sliding near the Chinese dancers. The dancers moved with rigid control, matching their steps to a long-practiced, long-remembered sequence of movements, a sequence that extended backward in time to the particular moments when sections of the dance had been formalized. These two dancers reproduced, in a corner of an Occidental park, a long line of moments remembered from generation to generation and now dissipated into the air above Riverside Drive.

The girls jumping along the hopscotch pattern looked deceptively spontaneous in comparison. Did they even remember the difficulty of the early steps? Or could it be that their bodies harbored a subliminal knowledge of those muscular arrangements that had taken eons to emerge as possibilities, ages in which the starfish was allowed his five-limbed radiancy, the bird its two gigantic wings, the mammals their four stable legs, the primates a relocated center of gravity; time had been needed for the hands to let go of the branches, for the primates to come down from the trees, their gradually developed buttock muscles tensing against the earth's great command—Fall Down!

The teacher and his pupil slowed almost imperceptibly but danced on, sending off to Sonya a kind of yellowness—China, sunshine—that spread to the edges of the park where the ruddiness of the children caught it and sent it back, their woolly sweaters bright, their cheeks and hands reddened. "Here we go, Alexandra," the blonde said, wiping raisin juice from the corner of the girl's mouth before lifting her out of the stroller. The dancers came to a halt almost simultaneously, plunged their sabers into their belts, and walked off.

Pathfinder

Victor felt his wife's slender hand on his shoulder and rolled over to face her. He ran the thickness of his palm down her shoulder, past her waist, over her hip.

"It's Saturday," she said, "your morning to get up. Don't you hear him?"

Then the din in his ears focused into words and he heard his son calling. He swung over the side of the bed and stepped onto the floor. "Your Daddy will arrive shortly!" he called through the open doorway in his lowest voice. Peter, startled by the sudden low tones, silenced himself and clung to the bars of the crib.

In the middle of brushing his teeth, Victor spit and called out through the bathroom wall in a falsified bass: "IN THE BEGINNING GOD CREATED THE HEAVEN

AND THE EARTH," and he added more toothpaste to his brush. "THE EARTH WAS WITHOUT FORM, AND VOID, VOID, VOID." Peter made no sound from the crib. "THE SUN, HE CAME OUT AND SHONE AND THE MOON LET OUT A LOT OF LIGHT." Victor spit again and pulled at the fuzzy clump of hair that grew above his ears. Still thick, maybe God listened to his morning song and so continued to bless him with hair.

"AND THEN, HE SAID, I'LL MAKE ME A MAN!" Victor swooped in upon Peter, who shrieked, giggled, and consented to be snatched from his crib. Victor searched in the refrigerator for the bottle Sonya had fixed the night before. He slipped Peter into his high-chair and handed him the bottle. He spread a little dry cereal on the tray and then sat on a stool himself, to down some toast and cheese and a slice of melon which he determined was not quite rotten enough to be too rotten. Cheese and melon, the combination reminded him of his long summer on the Irish coast. After twenty-mile bike rides with his fuzzy hair stuffed under a cowboy hat from the five-and-ten, he would sit under the eaves in his rented room listening to a transistor radio and slugging his way through Dante, "in the English," as his favorite professor had continually mocked the students of the classics. He enjoyed the seductive largesse of his landlady, who daily laid fresh cucumber and later, melon, on the unstable bed he

32

rented from her. Melon, late in the summer. Here it was spring and his son sat before him, sucking away at a bottle of milk. Guzzling, like his father, lusty.

"Sock it down, kid," he said to the replica of himself, but softly. A mess of diapers and pins, socks and sneakers, jeans and sweaters, and they were off, his son hanging over the edge of the stroller, examining the gobs of spit they rolled above as they wheeled toward the park. They passed beneath the balcony where a bald mannequin with bright red lips gave her somewhat waggish blessing to 8oth Street, the home of his thirties, the harbor of domesticity into which he had fallen. Klunk. Ah, red-lipped Beatrice, are you living here too?

"None of that playground stuff for us, kid," he said as they came to the park entrance. He examined a cryptic sign on which Mayor Lindsay appeared to be saying he might bounce a ball or smoke but could not spit or sleep. "With you and me, it's the wilds, strictly au naturel." Victor picked the boy out of the stroller and set him on his shoulders with the legs around his neck and the rump sinking over the top of his backbone. He collapsed the stroller, hung it from his right shoulder, and strode up a rocky rise with the boy clinging to his hair until they reached a place at the top that was wooded and green. The promontory gave him a view across rippled blue water. Into Jersey. "See!" Victor pointed. "Far shore! Enemy land!" The boy stared westward, unblinking, at Jersey, which rose in blank stone across the water and sent off whiffs of smoke: message, "Hoboken Tube, she arrive four minutes late."

Victor sat crosslegged on top of the hill and lifted the boy off his neck. Peter slipped and scraped his knee against some broken glass. He cried and Victor lifted the leg that was hardly longer than his own hand and sucked the scraped place. He spit out bits of sand. There was glass all over the rock. "Okay," he said, scratching the kid's head. "Let's go see the boats. We'll run for it." He gathered up Peter and the stroller and clambered down the far side of the hill.

They would go by secret path. Not one person must be allowed within fifteen feet of them. Difficult, but he had done harder things. He had walked all the way to midtown without once swerving from his determined path, scattering nubile biology majors like his wife and fairly crushing smartly dressed fellows like himself, other guys playing the same game of sidewalk dominance. Now he ducked behind a large tree to let a man and a dog pass at the set distance of fifteen feet.

He emerged from behind the tree and flipped open the stroller with one movement and set Peter in it. They rolled smoothly on a paved path. Suddenly a woman and girl came into view fifty feet off. Dangerous. He struck out to the left, through a stand of giant honey locusts. He flared his nostrils to increase the range of his smell but was met with the odor of still-warm dogshit. He narrowed his nostrils rapidly, stalking over the cracked earth. "Gonna lay down my sword and shield," he sang to himself. "Down by the riverside." He froze. A trio of nurses pushed their charges across a public path not far away. Too close for comfort.

He lurked in trees that bordered the esplanade. A jogger passed. Two boys on bikes. A girl on a two-wheeler with her Saturday parkbound father patiently explaining how she could keep her balance. Then the monkey lady appeared. She was far off at the start of the mall but walking directly toward him on a green avenue just inward of the trees. The monkey, wearing the diapers that his mistress insisted upon, skirted and flitted up trees. The woman smiled and waved to gawkers seated on benches along the mall as she progressed at her own slow, human pace. Her store-bought monkey whooshed down distances of twenty or thirty feet, hopped lightly onto her left shoulder, crossed the back of her neck, and launched off her right shoulder up ten or twenty feet of angled branch, rustling the waxy leaves and shaking the tender reaches of several trees at once.

Victor decided to make a break for it. He darted from beneath the locusts, touched the cement of the mall, pushed fast over the railroad grate hoping it wouldn't jar Peter's teeth, and safely reached the bicycle path that sloped down to the river. "We made it, fella," he announced happily. Peter smiled. Looking back, Victor saw that the monkey had reached the place where they'd been standing, the trees trembled now over the very spot.

Down the narrow path they headed, but before Victor could react, they were boomed past by a trio of boys on rev-pedaled bikes, silent, ominous, their presences tall, fast, powerful. Yet they couldn't have been more than thirteen or fourteen years old. Victor shuddered. Surprised. He hadn't heard them. The game was over.

Victor slowed down and began to show things to Peter. Flowers, grass, old and new leaves, the current in the river, a sailboat, a motorboat. The river passed from view as they entered a tunnel of foliage. They were alone on the downward path. What if armed youths should jump him? Would he resist? Against an unknown object disguised in a dirty handkerchief poked into his neck? What would he do? "Here's my money, fellows, would you mind terribly if I kept my credit cards?" But what would his son think of him when, hour by hour, he viewed Superman on Channel 11 striking back at evil, at least at crime? Suddenly the river came into view again. The water sunlit as he had loved it in the Mediterranean toward the end of the great European junket that had kept him from the army.

They reached the low level by the river wall, the cul-de-sac where Italian fishermen hung rods into the river. Women sat patiently on the benches with worn hands resting on picnic baskets. Not summer yet, but it was warm. Victor wiped the sweat off his forehead again and lifted Peter up to see the water lapping over a milk carton caught in the rocks.

"Good day!" Victor nodded to the old women.

"Beautiful," one said, "beautiful," pointing to the son who looked so like Victor with the coloring of Victor's Irish father—"an eye of the potato blight" as the old man had always described himself.

Me no Irish. Me no Italian. Me Indian. Me own land. Victor took his son's hand and they walked to the boat basin. He tried to erase Jersey, blot out the boats in the marina, destroy the man-imposed landscape of the park. Suddenly the landscape looked familiar, meadows, but with benches, a hillock. Then he remembered the same configurations from a wire service photo. Yes! Somewhere off to the left, near the knolls, a seventy-five-year-old woman had been murdered on a snowy afternoon, her blood staining the snow, the trifling contents of her stolen purse strewn about, her two poodles whimpering nearby—puzzled, patient, reliant on the world of men to snap or unsnap their chains, to look them in the eye, to say, "Your mistress is dead. You don't belong to her any more."

"Boats!" Victor pointed ahead and soon they were hanging over the railing watching boats bobbing on top of the water. They stayed until they got hungry and then made their way back over a shorter route to their own familiar exit out of the park. As they gained the top of the slope, Victor saw a collection of three or four people pointing at something and suddenly a chicken walked out in front of him.

"See him! There he goes!" shouted the people, all middle-aged, who gesticulated and pointed their long arms tipped with long fingers, and these with long nails, at the terrified chicken, who scurried about until it finally found refuge under a parked car. A few clucks and it was silent. "Dat?" Victor's son inquired. "Dat?"

Victor parked the stroller and braked it. He would show his son what it meant to be a man.

"What is it? What is it?" one of the middle-aged women was asking.

"It's a chicken," Victor answered, amazed that anyone would not know. He bent down to look under the station wagon that was sheltering the lost bird.

"A chicken! A chicken he says!" The questioner gasped.

Victor reached under the Ford.

"Oh, don't touch it!" another woman shrieked. "Don't you have a glove?"

"No, no gloves today," Victor replied, on his knees under the car. Actually, the bird was safer under there than it was on the street. Victor came out, stood up, uncertain. What would he do with the chicken if he caught it? Give it to Sonya to cook for supper? Maybe it was carrying diphtheria or sleeping sickness?

"The Puerto Ricans keep chickens right in their kitchens," chanted an old man bent over on a Riverside bench, mouthing the words tonelessly, as if he had been repeating them half audibly for two or three years, throwing the meaningless sounds out into the air, waiting for an event to come along and match them. Now that the event had finally occurred, he mumbled the phrase again and so magically began on the A.D. of his chant.

The ASPCA, Victor thought. He wedged a hand into a tight jean pocket and extracted his wallet in which was a dollar bill and one dime. "I'm going to call the ASPCA," he announced to the circle of admirers waiting for him to act. He ducked into a nearby phone booth, turning toward Peter so he could keep an eye on him while he called. He dropped in the dime. Nothing happened. He pounded on the phone box but just as he pulled down the return coin lever the dime fell behind it, lost to him forever. He pounded again, enraged, when he heard a pleasant voice asking him what he wanted.

"I want the number for the ASPCA," he said, "I'm on Riverside Drive and there's a chicken loose."

"A chicken?" the operator answered. "You're pulling my leg."

"Listen, baby," Victor heard himself saying. "I want the ASPCA. It's a matter of life and death."

The telephone operator riffled off into a beautiful sweet laughter but connected him with a ringing circuit that eventually identified itself as the ASPCA.

"You gotta catch that chicken first, buddy, and then, buddy, you can call us back. We don't chase no loose chickens on Riverside Drive." He hung up.

Call back without a dime! Catch a chicken! On a Saturday, at noon, with the sun shining on him and his son watching. But exactly, he couldn't have ordered anything better! He checked to make sure his son was watching and then he rolled up the sleeves of his sweatshirt and advanced toward the parked Ford.

"It's from a kosher butcher on Broadway," the crowd had decided. Victor stomped his feet beside the Ford. The chicken edged out and nervously scrambled up the curb onto the sidewalk and started down the slope toward the playground.

"Watch the boy, will you?" Victor called to his audience as he stalked the chicken.

"No gloves! He's got no gloves!" the woman shrieked again, stroking the leather covering her own fingers.

One, two, eight quick steps, a lunge, his hands circled to slightly larger than the dimension of the chicken—he had it, its heart beating fast and frightened beneath his fingers.

"Bring my boy, will you?" he called to a young couple with a stroller. The woman stayed with her own stroller while the man obeyed Victor, wheeling a transfixed Peter down the hill.

Gingerly, Victor dropped to one knee beside the stroller, extending his offering of a captive chicken.

"Dat?" Peter asked, quietly, his voice shrunken, his head pulled a bit away.

"That is a chicken," Victor said. "I caught it. I'm holding it tight." He decided he couldn't let go in order to guide Peter's hand to the quivering body.

"Touch it with your finger, here, near the back." He presented the chicken's rear. "Don't worry. I'm holding it."

Peter extended one hesitant finger and made the slightest of contacts. "Ha!" he gasped—the chicken started and Victor stood up. "Come on," Victor said, and started down the hill carrying the warm body that pulsed wildly.

Victor did not know where he was going. He passed through the gate on which Mayor Lindsay had neglected to post any remarks about chickens and spotted one of five or six wire wastebaskets scattered across the playground. There wasn't much in the first trash basket beside an old orange juice carton and some popsicle sticks.

"Empty it, can you?" he said to the man who was pushing Peter while Victor knelt to hold the chicken still on the concrete. The nylon-parkaed helper bent to empty the wire basket and then turned it smoothly over the chicken. The two men straightened up. They shook hands.

A man dressed in a brown uniform advanced from the door of the office attached to the comfort station and Victor told him the story.

"ASPCA? They'll never come on Saturday," the park man said. "Won't work overtime for anything this small."

"Well, I'm out of dimes," Victor repeated. "I'll call when I get home—I'll tell them I left it in your charge." The ASPCA didn't come on Saturdays? Someday maybe he could get them blasted on the six o'clock news.

The attendant indicated it was more likely that the chicken would be taken home for a pet than that the ASPCA would show up on a Saturday afternoon, but he promised to keep an eye on it. Victor pushed Peter up the slope toward the intersection on Riverside, nodded to the faithful audience and gave them a recap of the latest developments. He pointed down the slope toward the chicken that was trapped in the wire cage. "OOoh, oooh," they said in a chorus. Around the upturned basket children played and around them rose the larger circle of the fence that enclosed the playground, and even though the scene was sterile and rigid, gone from wildness, bound, Victor's heart was light.

On
and
Off
the
Warpath

There was a man in the baby park. Sonya stared. Her father and his colleagues in anthropology would have had a field day observing him. Why wasn't he among the warriors beating foliage on the way to the neighboring village? Was he unemployed? A loiterer? Pernicious? Vicious?

He was handsome. He had black curly hair and a dark blue shirt opened to reveal a bit of chest and he wore Levis and, below them, cowboy boots. His face had thin, regular features, perhaps a bit too fine. He must be under thirty or he wouldn't be babysitting on a weekday. He was deeply tanned but his nose showed shades of red under the tan. Was he an alcoholic? He smoked a lot. Space had been carefully left on the bench to either side of him and, although the women would not sit next to him, they kept casting eyes in his direction. Would he masturbate? One perfectly innocent fellow had sat a full hour on a park bench one Wednesday morning with his hands rigidly to his sides and three women had reported him to the police for masturbating.

The air was hot. The trees fully occupied—a green leaf at each node. At the height of August the human female population had dropped to one fifth its autumn or spring size. Most of the women went out of the city to oceans or lakes. Camaraderie among the heat-winnowed remnant increased. The ten or twenty white women who haunted the buckling asphalt morning and afternoon came to know each other very well and broke the age, class, and child-distribution barriers that kept like with like on separate benches during the cooler months.

Ah, the man had a son. The boy ran his tricycle into the bench where his father was sitting. The benches began to fill up and women sat on either side of the man. The cowboy, they came to call him, as the days stretched forward. The tide moved toward him gradually. Women found themselves striking poses with their arms and legs that they had never bothered with before. His daily entrance into the park caused a general stiffening that never quite left the environs; ventral aspects were generally presented in his direction.

Sonya stretched out the back of her neck to force

down her hint of a double chin, since she was separated from the cowboy by only the blond dancer, whose name she now knew was Nicole, and by Pauline, a drunken double mother—boy, two; girl, six months. Sonya opened an impulsively store-bought iced tea and Nicole unscrewed her year-round container of coffee. Pauline engaged the cowboy in the listening end of her non-stop complaint about child care, while she sipped on Scotch from a plaid thermos. "This one," she said loudly, contorting her face and indicating her son not three feet away, "is not only *dumb* but ill-*mannered*."

Sonya looked left over Nicole's bluejeaned knee and bare foot, across the laps of Pauline and the cowboy, to the patch of concrete where Peter was exploring.

"I'm seriously debating," Nicole said to Sonya, "whether I shouldn't move up to the 92nd Street playground, or over to Central Park and 85th."

"How come?" Sonya asked, watching Peter collect twigs.

"They have different ethics at Central Park—nearer the East Side, I guess." Nicole stirred her coffee thoughtfully.

"Different ethics? Do they bite or something?" A twig from the neat row Peter had aligned on her thigh slipped off and Sonya bent to replace it.

" 'We don't bite,' it begins, 'we don't borrow toys, we always share tricycles upon request, we don't hit, we never hit, we may lash out verbally, we may not hit!' " Nicole sipped conclusively.

45

"Classy," Sonya breathed. "And what about 92nd?" she inquired, still rearranging twigs while she watched Peter make his way to the steps of the slide.

"They're integrated," Nicole replied. "Not the nurses," she explained, indicating the isolated nurse-maids at the far end of their own benches, "but mothers, black mothers and kids."

Black kids! Sonya remembered the day last fall that a black girl had been playing on the mall and the white mothers had encircled her with ooohs and aaahs, joyfully presenting their toddlers to be integrated. Suddenly she noticed that Peter was swaying on the steps of the slide leaning backwards, and groping for the railing. Sonya jumped up and ran to the slide to stand behind him, with a hand outstretched but not touching, allowing him freedom.

Tony, the cowboy's son, threw himself between her left leg and the steps of the slide. He pushed eagerly up the steps, jamming his body against Peter's, who wavered atop the stairs.

"Take it easy, Tony," Sonya admonished. "It's Peter's turn." She grabbed for Peter's ankle to keep him in place while Tony ignored her and pushed around Peter to go down the slide. Then he ran off, the movements of the muscles around his backbone showing, since he wore no shirt.

Sonya let go of Peter's ankle and he settled himself slowly at the top of the slide. Maybe she was overdressing Peter, her son was wearing a long-sleeved shirt while the cowboy's son had none at all. Maybe she should roughen him up a bit, barefoot into the snows and all that.

She could hear Pauline's grating voice from the slide and she turned to watch the happenings on the bench. "Those newborns are pretty smart, too, they *know* how to catch a cold on a *Friday* night."

The cowboy made a sympathetic face, raising his lips in a kind of snort that revealed two upper front teeth shorter than the other teeth, the short two. gave him a juvenile expression. Tony dashed toward the sandbox.

"Say," Pauline's voice took on a kind of triumphant edge, "your kid looks cold, he's shivering. Didn't you bring a shirt?"

The cowboy searched in a nearby stroller. "Guess she didn't put one in," he answered, fetching a cigarette from the pocket of his Levis.

Pauline settled back with an air of virtue, having corrected a man. Sonya smoothed her hair behind her ears, realizing she'd been willing to do whatever the cowboy did, blindly. Nicole leaned forward to offer an extra sweater of Alexandra's but the cowboy declined it. Tony jumped into the sandbox and grabbed Alexandra's pail.

Peter slid and Sonya moved to the lip of the slide to be there when he slipped off the end. From that distance, she could not hear the conversation on the bench. She noticed the pregnant remedial reading teacher crossing the park with her son. Peter didn't need any help getting off the slide. He turned and started deliberately for the steps again. Sonya walked back behind him and stood while he climbed. She could hear the voices on the bench again.

"Hey, how do you like your Big Boy pants?" the teacher inquired of Pauline's son, whose training pants hung below his rompers. He didn't answer.

Sonya walked to the end of the slide again and smiled at Peter when he reached the bottom. "What a big boy you're getting to be," she said to Peter, remembering too late her vow never to invoke that loathsome fellow, the mythical Big Boy who was always a step ahead of living boys.

She walked back to the steps.

"How shall I prepare Jonathan for sibling rivalry?" the teacher was asking Pauline across the lap of the cowboy, while she set her baby on the cement. He crawled to the dirt by the tree.

"Sibling rivalry!" Pauline shrieked. "Listen, just get a *screen* for the top of the baby's *crib!*"

"Good heavens, Pauline, don't you listen for their inner fears and feelings?" the teacher admonished, directing her gaze reproachfully toward Pauline. "We have to know what they're thinking." Her baby fingered the dirt at the base of the tree, dirt full of glass and peach pits, and old cigarettes.

Sonya moved out of hearing to the front of the slide. Suddenly she heard Nicole shout and saw her jump up and run toward the tree. The eyes of the three on the bench were turned to Nicole but the bodies sat transfixed as Nicole grabbed the teacher's son and turned him upside down. Then the teacher ran over and screamed, "Are you all right?" at her baby, whom Nicole slapped between the shoulder blades. A strand of brown liquid hung from his mouth and then a cigarette butt fell to the ground. He gagged and screamed. Nicole handed Jonathan to his mother, who rocked him. His face was gray and he rested his head upon her shoulder, shutting his eyes.

Sonya reached for Peter's hand as they walked back to the steps of the slide. Another scream came, this time from the sandbox. Peter calmly climbed the stairs but Sonya swung around to see Tony smacking Alexandra on the head with a shovel.

"Leave her alone," the cowboy called from the bench. "She's just a girl."

Nicole walked over to the sandbox and removed the shovel from Tony's hand. "We don't hit girls!" she said sternly. "And we don't grab shovels!" She extracted the shovel from his hand and returned it to Alexandra.

Sonya walked to the front of the slide and saw Peter lose his balance midway down. His smile turned to a look of terror until he righted himself and ended his slide smiling. "That's a boy!" Sonya said, clapping him on the shoulder.

"Let's get out of here," Nicole appeared suddenly behind her. "The cowboy is telling Pauline that he picks up a few bucks between auditions giving the spiel on the Circle Line boats. I wish he'd get a job soon and get that kid of his out of our sandbox."

It was noon and Nicole and Sonya pushed their strollers together to Broadway, where men examined Nicole's seductive walk—a motion Sonya had practiced as a teenager but never mastered. They parted at 86th Street.

"Have you got a smile for your butcher today, Mrs.?" the red-nosed meat man whispered in his throaty cigar-damaged voice, grinning at her as he hacked at a leg of lamb.

"Anything for a leg of lamb," Sonya responded, reluctantly producing the smile without which there would be no boned chicken, no lean brisket, and no sale spareribs.

"Now how about a nice slice of baloney for the boy?" he asked, handing a bit of meat over the counter top for Peter.

In the dry cleaning store she leaned her hip against the counter and drew her chin under.

"That'll be two fifty," the dry cleaner's son said, examining her with eyes that looked as if they spent the steamy, Carbona-laden day in dreams of passion. At night he went to City College.

"Okay," she answered, gazing into his publicly non-committal eyes, wondering if he had a flesh and blood girlfriend and what they did with each other in the evening. Whatever it was, they probably did it in the middle of the night on the beach of a deserted Coney Island. Maybe Far Rockaway, after a long, excited ride on the E train.

"There you go, Ma'am," the boy said, handing her the change and pressing the plastic-wrapped garments into her hand. Their hands touched in the slightest way, at the edges of the palms.

Just before crossing 84th, Peter was offered a piece of gum by an old man in a Homburg hat. In the middle of the street, an old woman warned Sonya that Peter's fingers were too near the spokes of the stroller wheel. Near the farther curb she stepped over a puddle of water. It came from a Chevrolet that was waiting for the light to change. The man in the driver's seat sat impassively waiting for the traffic light while water ran out of his car radiator. Sonya stared. "Leak! Leak!" shouted a man near her, waving wildly at the hood of the car. The driver opened the door and leaned out to check. "Thanks," he called to the man in the street, and waved to him. It had never occurred to her to warn the man.

She passed the drugstore by for the second week; she didn't have money to buy new shampoo for herself, she would have to use Peter's again. Sonya approached the grocery store where she had a charge account. A very pregnant woman came out, her husband held the door open for Sonya; he examined Peter and exchanged smiles with Sonya as she pushed the stroller over the broken threshold.

"Things that gloomy, Miss?" the bad-breathed

grocery clerk inquired, leaning forward confidentially. She gave only a weak central raising of the brows, knowing what was coming. It always seemed to be coming.

"All I'm asking for's a little smile," he explained condescendingly. What right had he to ask her for a little smile? She ignored his request. "Put it on the bill," she said as she shoved a single milk in his direction and busied herself arranging a place for the milk in the stroller while she waited for her purchase to be wrapped and shoved toward her. Shooting a low score today, Miss, she admonished herself as she maneuvered the stroller out the double-doored exit.

Yet she remained resourceless when a garbage man near her own brownstone stoop looked up her skirt as she climbed the stairs and whistled "Lady Be Good," while she rose stubbornly higher and higher above him.

After Peter was down for his nap, Sonya ran the water for the dishes she had always so much hated to wash. She studied the water's circular motion toward the drain. She knew it followed the drag in the wind and water that turned from the spinning bulge of the equator in slow arcs toward the poles, clockwise in her kitchen, counterclockwise in Australia. It was evening in the great outback. Englishmen played cricket and drank beer while their wives sewed cancer pads. Inland, aboriginal men taught their sons the names of ritual stones or played games and drank homebrew in preparation for the next day's hunt that might or might not produce meat. Women mended their sandals for the morrow's walk over hot desert sands in a search that must result in the day's roots, nuts, and water—while the water sank into the earth so deep that sucking straws would scarcely reach it by dawn.

"I finally talked with the cowboy today," Sonya lied to Victor when, later that night, she stretched her bare thighs on top of the sheets that covered the brass bed. The fan at the window redirected a little hot air over them.

Victor sat at the desk in their bedroom, appearing to read *Panama*, in an armchair excursion he had not made for some months. He wasn't, however, actually reading, but staring at the checkbook on his desk. They couldn't live on his salary. Fourteen thousand had seemed like a lot, especially since his father had sent three children to college on half that. But since Sonya had quit work, they had spent their way through all six thousand dollars of their savings and he had today reached the bottom of the checking account.

"He was very nice," Sonya was saying, waving a thigh. "He gives talks on the Circle Line boats."

"Hm." What would become of them? His throat felt constricted. Sonya planned to stay out of full-time work for five or six years to raise the children herself and he was glad about that. But so far she'd only gotten two free-lance jobs, and they had paid a crummy hundred dollars apiece.

"It's nice to see a man in the daytime," she added. "Usually my masculine companionship is limited to the soft purring of storekeepers and passersby."

"Ha." He turned a page. He couldn't get involved talking now. He had to figure out what to do. The ski area had lost its credibility. Samson at the newsdesk had proffered two thousand, then retracted it when his daughter's first private school bill had come due. Nobody else had been interested, not even his brother the programmer.

"Yeh," he said in Sonya's direction, after registering an expectant silence on her part. What about a private expedition to the far north to stake out land for his family? The physical life in Alaska? Virtually alone in the snow, the King of Seward's Folly? Better than the Knave of Dobbs Ferry? No, there was nothing to do but push upward into the hectic production of TV programs, into the administrative posts that gave guys heart attacks. He was too loose for on camera, his enunciation too slurred. Besides, he had always suspected it would come to this, he knew his dreams of kingship served him only as a clever rearguard action, measures to distract the encroaching enemy while his front lines turned toward the hills. And his situation wasn't so bad, the urban life was comfortable, if cramped. Only the escape routes were being seriously damaged.

He turned another page, to a spread of native girls. Twenty tits, he counted them.

"What's that you're reading?" Sonya asked in a lowered voice.

"*Panama,*" he answered, clearing his throat. He rubbed his thumb across a Kodachrome breast. Smooth.

"Are you worried about something?" she asked him, quietly.

"No," he said, "it's just that I've renounced the physical life again." In the middle of life, I find myself at the gateway of . . . How did it go? Twenty tits, count 'em. He turned the page. Volcanoes.

The next day in the playground, Sonya resolved to make good her boast of the preceding night and actually talk to the cowboy, but the bench on either side of him was occupied. It was among the last days of the cozy summer park and the experienced mothers were waiting for some event to mark the change of seasons into the repopulation of autumn.

A man's shout filled the area and brought every woman to attention.

"You will let go! You little bastard! You will!" The cowboy shouted over the sandbox, trying to wrench a red-haired boy from combat with his son. He struck the red-haired boy, slapping with a hand big enough to cover half his face.

Eyes as distant as those of the nursemaids near the gate turned to watch. The boy dropped to the sand. His mother ran up. With an obscene gesture, the cowboy quieted her.

The red-haired boy was scooped out of the sand by his mother, who ran with him up to the street for a policeman. Pauline stuffed her kids into a two-passenger stroller; the seats next to the cowboy were vacated before he got back to the bench. The gaze which had been so magnetically drawn toward him was now deflected.

The leaves browned within the week and women returned to the city, swelling the population of the park, bringing fall outfits with fur collars, voices raised in greeting after the summer absence, and the raised volume of shouts that resulted from autumnal crowding in the sandbox. A new personage promised addition to the baby park as the pucci-scarfed woman presented a belly swollen in pregnancy, but the cowboy and his son were not seen there again.

In
the
Clearing

Sonya had managed to dress in her park best, a hand-some Irish knit pants suit, and to button her son into sweater and pants that matched each other; her house was clean, she had made both pudding and jello, and it was still early in the morning. She read her father's letter as she pushed Peter in the swing—"Since it is unlikely that you and your family will find time to visit us on the West Coast this Christmas, your mother and I have decided that we will visit you during . . ." She helped Peter down from the swing, where he now squirmed in boredom. She followed him leisurely across the playground as he made his way toward the slide and confidently slid each shod foot onto the steps that rose at waist-high intervals above him, using all fours when he reached the landing on top. There he swung his hind quarters out in front of his front quarters and plumped down to a sitting position. He looked triumphantly about the playground before he began to bang his shoes on the metal of the slide. CLANG. CLANG. Sonya had not expected a handsome child, but here he was, bending his knees at the bottom of the slide, yellow-haired and agile.

Indeed, Sonya had expected to live a bit in the solitary manner of Aunt Monica, whose photo album she had rediscovered the night before, askew behind books in her aunt's 1930's bookcase that Victor now claimed as his. The friable black pages of the album smelled like old hymnbooks as Sonya, sitting on the living room floor, had turned them—watching a steady procession of images of Monica among a changing cast of male companions. There were pictures taken by street photographers and in twenty-five-cent booths; there were poses Monica had snapped of men and poses men had snapped of Monica. There were family scenes from Oregon with Christmas trees and nieces and nephews and turkeys and babies—never Monica's —on the knees of Grandpas. It had been on just such a Christmas full of generations that Monica had first mentioned her series of cancer treatments that had proved unsuccessful and had taken Sonya aside, telling her it was time to leave her job on the paper in Portland and move east. She could live in Monica's apartment until she got settled. Monica would stay in Eugene among relatives. Sonya had left in early February. Although Monica had known a string of men, a fact the family made embarrassed jokes about, only one gentleman had telephoned Monica and not a soul had visited her from the east. She had never gotten back to New York, dying in March just as the winter rains came to an end.

In the album, some of Monica's men lasted four or five turns of the page and through seasons, appearing in their tweedy coats as well as in their tennis shorts. Only Monica was present long enough to show age. First the dating of her age by costume and then the aging of Monica's face and body progressed as Sonya turned page by page to the shock of the empty black sheets at the back.

Sonya put away the lonely and quietly decaying scenes of Monica's album. She took out her own jumbled contact sheets and the few enlargements she had stuffed between the pages of a red plastic album bought the week Peter was born. The pictures Victor and Sonya had snapped of each other gave way to the formal scenes of their wedding and then to the five-dollar portrait of Peter the hospital photographer had peddled to them a few minutes after his birth. There were so many pictures lying unpasted that some fell out when Sonya stood the album back up. This same jumble was beginning to show in her life, the cluttered furniture in the shrinking apartment, the uneven tempo of Peter's naps, her often frustrated attempts to snatch private time. Still, she moved from task to task during the day feeling that her hair was combed and her sweater buttoned, her stride, with a child giving her direction, finally matching the world's stride, her private pace not lagging behind or zooming ahead or veering off on a meditative solo as it had in the past.

CLANG, CLANG, CLANG, Peter's leather heels slammed against the slide and he pushed himself down without waiting for Sonya's presence at the foot of the slide.

"That?" he asked at the bottom of the slide and she followed him to the sunken sandbox. It was simple, suddenly they had abandoned the outskirts of the playground and moved into the thick of things. She fingered the camera in the outdoor bag to quell a touch of nervousness at being in the heart of the playground. The roll of film in the camera was already exposed, she had shot it on a free-lance assignment for the science text—twenty frames of water boiling in a glass pot on her stove. Nevertheless, when she was assured that Peter was happily if sedately ensconced in the pit, she raised the box to her eye to see what she could see in its time-stopping rectangle of abstraction.

The vision of women clustered about a homely Sicilian well returned to Sonya, and in the shadows of their garments lurked the females of a band of jungle monkeys huddled in a clearing lost amid dripping trees. Here in the rectangle appeared the adult females of a conglomerate band of city builders caring for not one, but two, young at a time. Captions rattled in her ear, speaking pedagogically in the sinister whisper of italic, in a tone not unlike the one that echoed from the monographs piled in her father's office in the university's anthropology department.

"This race of city-dwellers rears two young at a time—each offspring getting less attention than a newborn ape." Sonya focused on the women nearby. *"The tribe is mixed, but, on the whole, handsome. Most of the females wear a standard dress of tunic and flared pants, while many suspend colored discs before their eyes to deflect the sun's rays."* Sonya raised the lens to the farther stretches of the playground. *"One segment of the population is distinguished by a skin color different from that of the majority. Whether they are slaves, the loot of war, or simply hired servants is difficult to judge. Whatever the origin of their low caste, the fact that it is ascribed to them is clear—the job of caring for offspring other than one's own always correlates with youth/age or captivity. Another correlation exists between the realization of unhappy status on the part of the hired nurses and their location nearest the exit gate."*

Sonya turned the lens to the center of the playground. She had seldom pointed her camera at human beings, it was a new experience. *"As with other primates, the young males are larger and more nervous; here they are especially fond of riding small vehicles as they chase after one another. The young females are smaller, calmer, and less interested in handling objects such as balls, stones, or sticks, more given to activities involving the sensations of their bodies—skipping, jumping rope, or swinging a ball about their ankles from a string attached to a plastic ring."* Sonya's eye followed her ear to the source of screams as a woman slapped a boy with one hand and clasped an infant to her breast with the other. *"Quarrelsome juveniles engage in encounters with adult females—as well as with peers—as they try to work their way through and out of the female hierarchy and upward into the male. Infants still clutch at their mother's hair, ready for the speedy retreat of arboreal primates; they suck and press against female necks and breasts—the pleasurable sensations of infant care contribute to the stimulation of female erogenous zones, which, in turn, leads toward the production of further offspring."* Suddenly the noise level around Sonya shot up.

She lowered the camera to reveal the real world. The pucci-scarfed woman had wheeled her newborn baby into the circle. Her bench neighbors shouted greetings and jumped up to look inside the high-domed pram. *"The love of newborns reveals itself in the crowding of females around any addition to the population."*

Sonya's concentration was broken. She struggled to recapture it, raised the camera to her eye to view the excited scene before her. *"The top of the female hierarchy can be located by noise level."* The caption flagged to faintness against the louder sounds of children calling and of women chatting about the newborn, or screeching as they rescued and scolded. *"Here the teeth are seen more frequently in laughter or in speech,"* ran the caption slowly as it faded. Then the camera seemed to take possession of Sonya's hands and directed itself toward the gate in a desperate swan song. *"At the edges of the clearing the women of different color do not show their teeth."* The almost inaudible caption petered out entirely as Sonya swung the camera jerkily to her lap.

"Have you seen him?" someone asked Sonya and she replaced the camera in the outdoor bag. Reality returned to her surroundings and Sonya found herself walking over to the pram to peer at a pink-faced, black-haired baby boy born exactly a week earlier, at dawn.

As Sonya stood peering into the carriage, the foreman of the park peered out of the window of the office attached to the comfort station near the gate of the park. He flicked his cigarette into an old paper coffee container on the dirty windowsill and gazed across the cement toward the women gathered about the sandbox. He checked his watch and counted the number of children in the sandbox. He jotted the number down on a form—it was time to request new sand.

Sonya gave her congratulations to the new double mother and collected Peter and his sand pail, slipped him into the stroller, and left for home. Once through her brownstone's locked door, Sonya took off Peter's cap and sweater and rolled the stroller into the darkness at the end of the hall. She slipped an arm around Peter and carried him up the stairs, two flights were still too many steps for him. She set him on his feet at the top of the stairs, and, holding his hand so he wouldn't fall backwards, opened the door and led him into the apartment. Beautiful, her son, her house, her new pants suit. She fixed Peter and herself a perfect little lunch and showed him a perfect little picture book where he pointed perfectly and accurately, even remembering the world "Fouse!" for flowers; she laid him to sleep in the crib.

She leaned over the crib rail, watching; once she had leaned out from the back seat of her family's car as they drove to their vacation in the mountains and she'd seen an old woman sitting on a porch, used up, her puffy hands resting on her lap. If the old woman had wonderful things to remember, age would be acceptable. Perhaps Sonya was moving in wide circles toward that porch in the mountains, toward the old woman in the chair, and she wanted to take with her the sight of her son at this minute, now, as he lay obediently in his crib, returning her gaze, wondering what her next move would be, feeling himself near sleep without knowing what sleep was, shutting his eyes, opening them to make sure she was still there. Finally he did not open them.

Sonya snatched up the camera which contained the frames of the water boiling on the stove and vanished into the closet. Behind the winter clothes, her shoulder pressing against the stored skis, she stood reeling film into a developing box and trying to think about something other than mothballs, when she heard the phone ring. She could never make her heartbeat slow down at the sound of a ringing phone. But she couldn't leave the blackness to answer it without destroying the images not yet permanently captured on the film. And she couldn't reel while the phone rang. Any interruption in the reeling process always made her forget the delicate chronology of left and right turns, of ups and downs, that only six years ago her fingers had learned to do consecutively in the dark. The phone had now rung fifteen times. It wasn't Victor, he rang a maximum of five times, knowing that if she didn't answer by then she had the baby diaperless or was preventing him from choking. Was it her office reminding her about the deadline for the heat photographs? Was it Nicole from the baby park? Had her father been taken to the hospital? After the twentieth ring there was silence. Miraculously, Peter had not woken up. With the quiet, Sonya could concentrate again and she finished reeling. Later, in the bathroom, where the negatives hung from the shower rail, Sonya was fiddling with the enlarger when the phone began to ring again. This time she could leave the room without disturbing anything. She hurried to the kitchen phone and took a breath: "This is a recording," she said, as tinnily as she could. "When you hear the beep, please leave your name and number and your call will be returned. *Beep!*" She listened while Victor's unmarried sister spoke her name and number. Things weren't so bad, why did the park women complain so much? All it took to grab a little private time was ingenuity.

She finished with the enlargements, floated them in pans of chemicals in the bathtub and cleaned up the luncheon dishes. She was happily seated at Aunt Monica's cherry desk, moved from the former darkroom into the hallway, trying to figure out how to show molecules in motion, when the phone in the kitchen rang a third time. Victor.

"Did you hear from the doctor?" he asked.

"He said anytime was okay," she answered, smiling, though Victor couldn't see.

"Good," he said, sounding pleased. "What did you do today?"

"Went to the park. I'm doing my free-lance project now."

"Photographing heat again, Mrs. Galileo? Not so easy, but for my Sonya, an ordinary day." His lovely, intelligent Sonya who could rear babies and shoot molecules with one hand behind her back. Bang! How much were they paying her this time?

"Hey, listen to this," he suddenly remembered the ad in the apartment section, which he scanned every day now, although the monthly rents were usually half his salary. "Three bedrooms in Yorkville, a view of the river, elevator building . . ."

Sonya's mind wandered off to the papers on her desk. "Steak au poivre?" she heard herself saying. It must be what they'd be eating tonight.

Peter was perfect at supper and Sonya had time to get sherry glasses ready, and a little cheese.

"Daddy!" he screeched when Victor's steps were heard on the stairs and his key in the lock. Victor stumbled into the hallway in an attempt not to step on Peter, who was throwing himself at the door, and, at the same time, to be ready to catch him in case he should project himself out the door and down the stairs.

"Peter!" Victor swung the boy up and Sonya kissed Victor. It was seven fifteen, Victor was usually home by seven.

They put Peter to bed together, Victor zipping him into his pajama bag and Sonya sitting on the toy chest, sipping her sherry. They sang to him, the lullaby they had learned when Peter was still in the womb, Victor leaning close over Sonya's abdomen to sing because she'd read a fetus can hear at seven months. Darkness at the windowpane of what was once the darkroom, brightness inside, colored paper, mobiles, paintings, stripes, dots, puffy pillows, rugs with animals on them. Perfect, it was all perfect.

Sonya set the table by the living room fireplace

with candlesticks and silverware and seared steak au poivre with French beans. They ate while music reached them from Aunt Monica's very old but very good phonograph. After supper they made love on the living room couch, the door couch that had once belonged to Victor alone, and before Peter awoke in the morning, a second child had been conceived. A girl.

Safe!

Snow circled the base of the oak tree near the entrance to the playground. The park foreman heard a click as he unlocked the office door by the comfort station. Sounds traveled faster in the dense air of winter. He peered at the thermometer before opening the door— seventeen degrees. When he was seated at his desk, he figured out and recorded an average February temperature of twenty-four degrees.

The air began to warm, to show elasticity. In March the five young of the eastern gray squirrel inhabiting a nest in the oak by the playground were carried from the darkness of the womb into the air and light, a light that did not register on the blind eyes of the half-inch-long squirrels. Rains carried off the snow and revealed a sodden circle of leaves beneath the oak. Harder, relentless rains threatened the shabby nest of bark and needles the pregnant squirrel had hurriedly thrown together in a notch of the tree.

She grasped the stomachs of the young in her mouth. They wrapped their tails and legs around her neck and the group fled the watery nest together. The mother searched over a neighboring oak, finally poking her head into a den in a hollow of the tree. Inside the den was another female with a litter. And three unrelated males. The mother entered and was welcomed by animals made friendly in the desperation of winter. The rains continued and finally removed the snow from the ground in which the few remaining acorns and hickory nuts lay buried. The squirrels ate the last of the nuts, waiting for the first fruits and berries to appear.

"Look at the squirrels, how thin they are!" Sonya wheeled Peter to a lookout over Riverside Drive where squirrels ran between trees.

"Squirrels," she said again, slowly. "Thin," she pointed to their tails. "Hungry, they are hungry," she kneeled beside the stroller. Peter leaned over the stroller pointing, his arm chunky in the heavy snowsuit. "Squirrels," he repeated. "Hungry."

The park foreman opened his office window a crack, set his coffee on the desk, opened his ledger, and recorded an average March temperature of thirty-one degrees.

. . .

Light appeared from the direction of Riverside Drive, spilling onto the surface of the river. During the darkness, auxin in a seedling had fallen toward the gravitational pull of the earth, dragging the root inward, positioning the seed so that the green shoot would creep outward toward the soft, wild freedom of the air. Light flowed steadily from Fifth to Broadway to the Hudson Parkway, repelling auxin in the green leaves, sending it to the dark side of each leaf, where it brought growth as the underside of the leaf swelled and curved, stretching the upper side to bring the largest surface of food-making green to the light.

"Leaf," Sonya said, lifting Peter in his sweater from the stroller. She grasped him in one arm, and pulled the branch of a tree down with her free hand. The boy's fingertip was soft, its inner structure still of cartilage; the bone would not develop until full growth was obtained. He touched his fingertip to the bud.

"Soon there will be many leaves on the trees," Sonya added, swinging her arm to include the whole barren clump of trees about them. "It will be warm soon. It is spring."

"Spring," the boy repeated, an abstraction. She usually tried to avoid abstractions, but this one she couldn't resist and smiled to hear him say it, though tears came into her eyes, too.

· · ·

With spring, the light increased and rain continued to fall on the artificial park; the land flushed green. The light and the greenness came to rest on the light-sensitive cells of the eyes of a pair of pigeons inhabiting a small area inland of the river. Hormones raced to the testes of the male and to the ovaries of the female. The sperm-producing and egg-storing organs swelled. The male, with the female following, took to the air for a short flight to locate a nesting site. The male alighted near a low bush and the female, her abdomen swollen with unfertilized eggs, came to a stop and established herself on the site chosen by the male. She claimed it for the pair while he flew off to find nesting materials. He returned time and again with twigs and leaves in his beak which he dropped at her feet. She rearranged them and slowly built a nest around herself.

When the nest was built, the male began to sing and dance. As the female watched, her pupils widened, and as they widened hormones arranged for the release of two eggs from her ovaries. Once the song had begun, the sequence of events took on a carefully timed, lock-step order, for, even though this pair had mated the preceding season, there was danger that the transfer of sperm from one lightweight body to another would go wrong.

He put his bill into hers. She put hers into his. He

watched as she tilted her body forward, making her back level. He fluttered behind her, flapping his wings to keep his balance. She raised her tail, he saw the opening beneath. He lowered his tail, pressing it forward and beneath the underside of his body. He had no cock, only a lipped opening from the body cavity. He brought the underside of his tail forward to touch hers. Sperm passed over safely in less than a second and swam into the female tract, which led to the descending egg cells. The pigeons disengaged, preened, and ruffled their feathers.

In two days, a white egg left the warmth of the female body, but she stood over it in the nest, providing a roof of heat. When a second egg lay in the nest, she sat over the two. The male flew off for food. When the sun was halfway to zenith, the male rested on the nest and the female took her turn at searching for food until the sun dropped halfway to setting. Squirrels attacked the nest but timing was good; the hormones dictating defense of the young were still active in the bodies of the parent pigeons and they managed to send the squirrels whickering away. After the infant pigeons finally broke open their shells eighteen days later, they were fed a fatty food that seeped from the crops of both parents. But in a week the young were ready for larvae and insects, a body weight's worth per day. Unlike wilder birds, the city parents did not die of exhaustion or disease. Old ladies showed them the true abundance of the polar spring by scattering bread on the pavement.

.   .   .

"Green, Sonya, the color of hope on this fine Sunday, if you have chanced to receive the background of a Roman Catholic from your Uncle Henry," Victor walked slowly as he gave Sonya an arm and she leaned against him meditatively, preoccupied with the flutterings of life in the womb. It was indeed Sunday, the day when couples turned out to the esplanade to display mates or children in a way of reassurance: "Here is mine," and "I see yours," and "Aren't they fine this year?"

"I'm sure God has a sense of humor about all this," Victor gestured to include the entire landscape. "Easy come, easy go." Sonya clasped Victor's muscular forearm. She loved walking with him in dangerous, public places. She felt he'd be able to defend her against armed thugs.

"You'd better rest," he said, laying a hand on her abdomen. "We'll have to walk back fast to get there by the time we promised the sitter." He didn't want to have to pay her extra, either. He settled Sonya on a bench. Sonya's arms folded above her hardened abdomen. She thought of the madonnas in the museum. There weren't any with two children. No second, haloed face peeking out over the shoulder; a woman had one child. A man hung in death or was being buried. There was fresh new grass behind the bench. It smelled sweet.

. . .

After the summer solstice, the cream-colored flowers of the linden blossomed, sending off a sweet fragrance. Pollen fell into a yellowish dust at the base of the trees. Sperm cells that reached the ovaries of blossoms and fell down self-built tubes were drawn closer and closer by the huge mass of the egg cell; they fought through the cell wall toward the force that pulled them.

The sun sent warmth, day after day. The warmth rode in the air, penetrated the earth, and shook up the soil, sending currents through the water. The park attendant noted an average of fifty-one degrees for June.

Peter finished an ice cream bar. Yellowjackets buzzed near the remnants of ice cream on his lips. Sonya shooed them off.

"Bad this year," she remarked to Nicole, whose daughter quietly laid her hand on Sonya's belly.

"I saw the cowboy on Broadway this morning," Nicole said. "He was stoned, leaning against the cafeteria."

"I'd forgotten all about him," Sonya replied, reaching for a ladybug on her ankle.

"Peter," she called. "Ladybug, ladybug, fly away home." He followed the beetle, on his haunches.

"They smell so wonderful," Sonya and Nicole agreed, looking up from their benches toward the fragrant trees.

"Over at 85th Street, it stinks," Nicole said. "They've got a ginkgo there, a female. Imagine that! They've got a male tree and a female tree! The female smells of vomit every other fall." She reached to restrain Alexandra's hand. "Gently," she said. "Gently."

Sonya felt a movement pushing out her abdomen, she turned her face downward and saw a lump moving beneath the blue maternity blouse that was too tight.

In July, under the linden trees, a human embryo responded to the commands of hormones. Its heavy head was pulled earthward, sinking into the pelvic cavity. Locked in place, the baby quieted. In a day or two there would be danger, strangeness replacing familiarity. Sonya sat quietly on the bench beneath the trees. The heat was oppressive; it seemed to press upon her body and contain it.

"Thunder," she heard Nicole say, but through a veil of heat so heavy that Sonya imagined a sound-photograph of Nicole's voice, saw the movement from the voice box slap molecules of air all the way across the space that separated Nicole's mouth from her own ear. She saw the force of the voice zigzagging and diffusing, shimmering in the heat and being thrown back by the heavy air toward the speaker's mouth. "Thunder," Sonya repeated, as if to superimpose her word on Nicole's and rescue it. She felt heavy, immobile, a permanent part of the bench on which she sat, never to move again, to turn brown and yellow in the autumn, to be covered with a layer of snow in the winter, to bloom green next spring, enduring through season to season, herself.

Shiftings

The two-week baby nurse was small and nutlike, charm-
ing, courteous but suspicious-looking. Sonya arranged
to get the baby away from her and Peter into his nap,
where he would sleep until late afternoon, when, before
clocking her day off, the nurse would dress him and
bring him to the park to meet Sonya. Alone with the
week-old baby, Sonya skirted the entrance to the playground and headed, instead, to the outer, quieter
reaches of the green stretch along the river. She pushed
the big carriage under a shade tree and braked it addi-
tionally with the aid of a few stones before she settled
herself on one of the new baby's receiving blankets
spread carefully on the grass to avoid a hard lump of
dogshit and a broken bottle. She ate a peach and tossed

the denuded pit into the bushes, listening as bees buzzed and birds sang and the warm smell of summer foliage eddied around her. She set the refrigerated bottle of milk into the spot of sunlight reachable where she stretched her hand and watched as beads of moisture formed on the outside of the bottle. She lay down on her stomach, curved into a semi-circle trying to keep the upper part of her body on the small blanket. Free, her body was her own again. The ants that ran around her ankles were welcome to what they could get.

He had always been horizontal or sitting. She was always on her feet, had been vertical for virtually the last two months of pregnancy. Standing at the sink, stove, counter, crib; leaning over the tub, clearing the table, the toy-strewn floor; corny sciatica pains shooting down her thighs, her abdomen stretched and heavy, her feet with their fallen metatarsal arches, resting wrong on the floor, making her legs ache. She was the one who should sit, not Victor. Or lie down. She couldn't even get a seat on a bus from a man despite the fact that her abdomen stuck out so far it indented a fellow's newspaper as he read. Women would give her seats, usually. Especially black women. The only seat she'd gotten from a man had been offered when Victor was with her, and it was out of sympathy for Victor that the seat had been given.

Then she had lain down on the labor bed, been moved to the delivery table, and then to the mechanical bed in the corner of the rooming-in unit. A visiting husband had opened the window in the maternity room and a breeze had come in off the river. The current of air swayed the heavy cotton curtains hanging from railings around the four beds. It strengthened, and rattled the shade against the window glass. The sky darkened and the new babies, two, three, ten hours out of the womb, startled, woke, and gave little cries as a mid-afternoon clap of thunder threatened a storm that never materialized.

Only last week, one week ago, her daughter had been born. A girl was different. Herself. Small. More complicated to see herself redesigned, recollected, given a fresh start. Amassed into a new ball of potential, all that had gone into making her *plus* all that had been put into Victor's genes. That must be a multiple of some kind, some giant, vibrating statistic. Herself—only Italian. Irish wasn't so different. But Italian, southern? Herself as a southern princess rather than a maiden from the north. Goodbye Thor, hello Ali Baba, Lorenzo de' Medici, sunny skies, whores, arias. Would her daughter be a singer? And at her first concert, as her voice floated beautifully out over the orchestra, would Sonya's throat narrow, her voice vanish, stifled, held below, pressed down, destroyed?

"Oh, no, I never get post-partum depressions," Sonya had said languidly in the maternity ward and shut her eyes, hoping her guests would deposit the gifts and vanish. Now, a dog nosed around Sonya on the grass, but left, disinterested, and she dozed a few minutes until the baby wakened and produced faint cries of hunger, whereupon Sonya fed her the milk from the bottle and returned the infant to its carriage for the trip to the playground.

It was strange to take one so small onto a cement circle only lightly shaded and rebounding with noise. The carriage, supporting only eight pounds of baby and a few ounces of mattress bounced nimbly down the incline in front of Sonya, who searched for and spotted Peter and the nurse through the metal webbing of the fence.

As she pushed the carriage into the playground, several women jumped up.

"She's got the baby!"

"Let me look!"

She parked the carriage and displayed her sleeping daughter while Peter stood by, observing the notice given his sister. That the bench women were double mothers could be judged by the speed with which they shifted their repartee.

"Show me your sister, Peter!"

"What a beautiful baby you have, Peter!"

He still hung back. The women, including Sonya, resettled themselves on benches; the sky was heavy, the air humid. Sonya rocked the carriage gently with one hand and answered questions about the birth, while

Peter played a short distance from her, for the first time without being intently watched.

"God will watch you, Peter," Sonya thought cynically and yet hopefully. The Great Babysitter might come through, at that. Where did the sense of being watched from heaven come from? From mothers, perhaps, looking out of windows, through branches, across clearings, the children always aware of existing within another's vision.

The scene looked familiar yet strange, in that Sonya had been absent from it for a week. Things were moving rapidly; she squinted her eyes to keep out the sunlight. The whole day could be speeded up, starting with a view of the trees, alone, at the opening of day, and then the early arrivals, playing isolated games of ball or producing loud, virtually unheard clangs on the slide. Then the increase in population as ten and then twenty children shared the park equipment until the blue of the benches became obscured by the bodies sitting on them. Then the rise in sound level, the sweepings by park attendants, leading into the diminishment before noon. The noon whistle would blow and emptiness would follow, a vacant playground that even dogs deserted. The quiet of the siesta would lengthen, the sun slip past zenith and a few children would return with pretzels, ice cream, and then more and more children and adults, screams, thrown pretzels, dripping ice cream, frenetic activity, blood flowing, scraped chins, movements of elbows and knees, until toward

83

six the thinning of the population as at the edges of random ball displays, and then slowly, the quiet and the dark, the trees standing over their paving stones. Sonya found her eyes following Peter.

He seemed to be deflating in front of her eyes. Once, when she glanced at him, he had looked much older, like a schoolboy, and lonely. He began chasing a ball that five- and six-year-olds were kicking to each other. The older children ignored him completely. Sonya left the carriage and followed Peter, who was hurrying after a mass movement of older children. They reached the jungle gym like a school of fish and turned suddenly, leaving Peter still throwing himself toward it. Sonya found a ball and encouraged Peter to play with her and the two of them played ball in the middle of the playground. It was very hot and nobody else was venturing out into the unshaded circle. She felt weak, her stitches stung, the sun was making her lightheaded. She felt herself bleeding. She went back to rest on the bench. The baby cried and she rocked the carriage as she sat on the bench.

The first drops of the day's expected rain fell. The women stood, collected the children and their belong-ings, and hurriedly shepherded them off. Suddenly the playground was empty. Sonya picked Peter's raincoat off the bench where the nurse had placed it. Slowly she wheeled Olivia's carriage under the roof of the comfort station, out of the light rain which had miraculously cleared part of the sky of clouds so that the sun shone from time to time as the rain fell. Peter was dubious about the rain and clutched his rain hat to his head as he followed Sonya. They walked back to the jungle gym, leaving the carriage under the shelter.

Teenagers had come into the playground. A boy and a girl were already kissing under a tree and a bunch of adolescent girls under one umbrella stood by the seesaws, while a pair of adolescent boys on a bench listened to a transistor radio and stared at the girls across the playground. The music and the rain filled the space between the boys and girls.

Sonya chased Peter under the jungle gym. He wanted to swing from the bars and she discovered that in the short time since they had last played there he had learned to hang by his arms on the lowest bar and now he did it again and again, leaning his head back, making his rain hat fall off. From where she stood within the bars, setting his rain hat back on his head again and again, Sonya noticed that his wrists had grown below the place where she had turned up the sleeves of his slicker at the beginning of the rainy season. She had missed this growth, concerned with pregnancy and birth. She reached through the monkey bars to turn his sleeves down.

Bad
Day
At

"It's Livi," Victor was saying in her ear. Sonya opened her eyes. It was dark.

"Huh?"

"She'll wake up Peter. You better get up." Victor turned over.

Sonya set her legs onto the floor. They ached. She glanced at the clock. Her legs had had four hours' sleep, five the night before. Maybe if she did her exercises more faithfully, they wouldn't need sleep.

It was too late, Peter was crying. She fumbled across the crowded hallway, inching her way between the corner of the table and the playpen, into the children's room. Sonya picked up Livi, her knee buckling with the first, unbalanced weight. By sound she

87

realized that Peter had arrived at the top of his crib
railing, ready to throw himself forward into the void,
and she grabbed him in the other arm. They were
heavy, the baby in her right arm, the two-year-old in
her left.

"It's all right, Peter. You get down." He didn't
object and slid down her body, lying on the rug beside
his crib, and quieted. Sonya fed Olivia in the rocker
beside Peter, wondering why the baby had wakened
before dawn. Olivia seemed to be playing with the
bottle, not hungry. Sonya gave her an exasperated, evil
look. Cannily, with the hindsight of natural selection,
Olivia smiled at her mother and, soothed, drank. Sonya
rocked. The sky was just lightening when she settled
the children back into their beds and lay down on her
own beside Victor. Milk, she thought, as soon as her
head got to the pillow. We need two regular for Olivia,
two skimmed for Peter, and Victor wants more snacks.
She would telephone the market early in the morning,
sitting calmly at breakfast while she completed a
gourmet grocery list.

At seven thirty she was doing nicely, Peter was eating
his toast and she was buttering hers. Peter stood up in
his chair abruptly and continued to eat while urinating
through his diaper—there had been no dry rubber pants
available—over his legs, feet, the chair, and the floor,

including the steps of his kitchen stool and into the cracks where the rubber joined the metal. Sonya kept buttering her toast. If she didn't eat her toast now, she might lose her chance.

No good, she had to mix the orange juice before Victor reached the kitchen. She turned to the paper dispenser for towels to wipe the urine, but when she raised the cover of the dispenser the bare cardboard of another denuded roll of paper was revealed. She remembered her vow to refill everything when it ran out and started for the hallway closet where the towels were kept, but Peter was picking up his feet nervously, saying "Wet, wet," and so she held his hand instead and wiped the chair dry with a dishtowel. The kettle whistled as Victor walked into the kitchen; he hated a whistling kettle.

"I'll make some juice," he offered.

"I've got it! I've got it!" She rushed to quiet the kettle and then to the refrigerator, Victor's entry into the kitchen unsettling her, making her feel like an employee rather than a plant foreman. It had been that attitude on the part of her mother, and her mother before her, that had led a drunken Aunt Monica to proclaim to Sonya one Christmas Eve, "I married a violin instead of a concertmaster."

"There's your toast," she called over her shoulder, indicating the two pieces she had been buttering for herself. Victor sat on a stool and bit into her toast.

The juice concentrate was frozen solid and she

opened the can to let it warm a little. She must remember to buy wide-mouthed jars so she could dump frozen juice without waiting. She put in a third pair of bread slices to toast. But the trouble with wide-mouthed jars was that the heavy cardboard lining their lids turned moldy after many washes; but if you took the moldy cardboard out, the juice leaked when you shook the jar. She picked up dishes to put in the sink.

"Toast is burning, I'll get it." Victor did not move from his chair, but turned the *Times* over on his lap.

"I've got it," Sonya found the toast stuck and she turned her body so as to hide from Victor the fork with which she pried the wickedly crumpled pieces of toast out. (Why did Raisin crumple, while White did not?) Victor insisted she use wooden tongs to avoid electrocution and they were always lost. She buttered the toast and spooned gobs of chunky orange juice into a narrow-mouthed bottle and watched as some ran over the sides. She reached to wipe her hands but remembered the vanished paper towels and walked to the hallway closet. She kept the paper supplies behind the sheets and towels and the tumbled mess that greeted her eye brought to mind her mother's immaculate linen closet, each piece of linen folded with the rounded part of the fold facing the viewer. The better to wipe you with, my dear. The phone rang. "I'll get it," she called, snapping up a roll of paper towels in one blind reach behind the junky pile of sheets, before she shut the door.

It was long distance, her mother calling to remind

her to send an anecdote about her father for the "This Is Your Life" scrapbook that was being presented to him upon his retirement from the university. The phone woke up the baby and she began to cry in the specially designed cradle that stood at right angles to the living room couch and was waiting to be vacated and turned into a magazine rack.

"Livi's crying," Peter said.

Victor did not answer him.

"Livi's crying!"

Silence.

"LIVI'S CRYING!" He pushed his orange juice off the table.

"Yes," Sonya said, interrupting her phone call. "Livi's crying."

Sonya hugged the receiver to her shoulder, unrolled some paper, and bent to sop up the spilled juice. She wondered how many gallons of liquid she would absorb by one means or another that day. Her mother mentioned some details of the arrangements for the retirement party and hung up. *Tell what Dad said about the female brain when Mother found mistakes in the textbook he was writing,* she wrote on her reminder pad by the phone.

"Hey, Sonya! Will you tell that maid I give twenty dollars a week to stop hiding my bathmat?" Victor called from the bathroom. His bathmat, everything in the house belonged to Victor now.

Three cans of water for orange juice. Four and a half for lemonade. Three for grape. The doorbell rang and when Sonya opened the peephole she saw the long-awaited face of the super, come to fix the slow leak at the base of the toilet. "Have him come back in twenty minutes, will you?" Victor asked, his face soaped. Sonya waved a wistful goodbye to the vanishing super.

"Need any money?" Victor asked as he passed through the hallway wrapped in a towel. She was crouched on the floor changing Peter. Olivia had quieted and gone back to sleep, her desperate little cry still so delicate that it had slipped below Sonya's battered plea threshold. But Peter's lungs were larger and his voice piercing as he screamed an inch from her ear. She could barely hear Victor.

"I don't know," she said. Peter continued to scream.

"Well, how much do you have?" Lately Victor had not been too entertaining in the A.M.

Sonya did not know where her pocketbook was. Peter squirmed out of her hands and she caught him and carried him to the crib.

"Help me with my cufflinks, will you, babe?" Victor called from the bedroom. He had been looking neater lately, part of his job plan. Another few weeks and he should know whether he'd be an associate producer next season or not.

"I'll be right there." She grabbed the corner of Peter's diapers with all the strength she had and silently cursed as she drove the blunted pin through the layers of cloth into her thumb. Peter started to kick. She decided to risk another few minutes without rubber pants for Peter and set him on the floor. She wanted to get to Victor before his cufflinks did. On her way out of the children's room she stooped to pick up a diaper from last night and saw the black urine mark it had left on the floor. Rat's ass.

"I'm coming, Victor," she called and as she entered their bedroom to help with the cufflinks, she saw that the television pattern was moving vertically out of view. She reached for Victor's sleeve.

"Never mind," Victor said. "I did them, can you fix the TV?"

It was his own channel.

Sonya hated to fix the TV, and she wasn't any good at it.

"I can't ever do it right," she said, starting to make the bed. "Will you?"

"I don't have time." Victor sat down on the bed to tie his shoes, exactly where Sonya was straightening the bedclothes.

"I fix TV! I fix TV!" Peter called as he hit the television tube with his plastic hammer.

"Don't hit the television set," Sonya said, moving expertly away from the rumpled bed and grabbing the plastic hammer from Peter. She managed to slow the

93

vertical slip to a few fleeting changes. Instead of flowing steadily upward into the sky and out the solar system, the screen simply gave a kind of lurch every now and then and replaced the picture on the screen with an identical one that emerged silently out of the floor and fitted itself into the waiting square.

"Well, what about the money?" Victor was tying his tie in front of the full-length mirror and managing to emerge as his new unruffled, well-groomed business self. Sonya tried to piece together what cash the day would require.

"The money! Sonya! What about the money?" Victor was readying his wallet for insertion into his jacket pocket.

"Oh, I guess about ten," she said.

"Guess!" he cupped her breast, making sure that Peter wasn't watching. He leaned toward her, jokingly: "A man slaves all day to bring home the cash and a woman can't even anticipate expenses!"

"Ten, I need ten," she answered, moving away. If she asked for twenty he would want to know what she planned to spend it on. A hundred and he would laugh.

Victor handed her the ten, and Peter, realizing that the daily exchange of paper which signified his father's departure had taken place, began to cry.

"What's the matter, fella?" Victor scooped Peter up against his clean suit and then thrust him at Sonya. "He's wet!" he explained.

"Goodbye," Victor kissed her, pressing Peter against her clean shirt.

As Victor went out into the hallway above the stairs, he handed her the wastepaper basket, set out the night before for the super to empty.

Sonya bent her attention on getting outdoors. Did Victor really have to get to the office at nine now to bone up on producing? Or was he just getting out of the house? She was ashamed to ask. A lady's magazine quiz she'd read last month at the dentist's had raised the possibility that she might have paranoid tendencies. She rinsed diapers until the doorbell rang and, crossing the hallway to answer it, she decided to be rash; and so she flung open the door without checking in the peephole. The diaper man. She might have known. When she had received the diapers, she began a frantic search for her pocketbook, remembered seeing it earlier on a chair under the dining table that was now located in the hallway, and then, when she got it, remembered the ten was not there but in her apron pocket. She grasped the pocketbook in her left hand and fetched the ten from her pocket with her right. She took the change and shut the door behind the diaper man, still clutching the pocketbook. She kicked aside the plastic bag of clean diapers that blocked entrance to the kitchen and set the purse on top of the breadbox. Well done, that would be its permanent place. She tried to make one long-term household improvement per day.

Looking down, Sonya was happy to see that the urine on Peter's chair had dried, putting itself into the cleaning lady's province. She set on the kettle, slipped in new toast, and ran water over the dishes. She buttered the warm toast, took the grocery list off the hook, and perched on a stool. She tried to call to mind what she needed to replace in her refrigerator. She started in its freezer: pizza, frozen juices. Its hinged door: apple juice, capers. Its depths: sour cream, berries. Its drawers: endive.

The phone rang and woke up Livi.

"Hel*lo*," Sonya answered.

"What's the matter?" It was Victor.

"Phone woke up Livi." Sonya sipped coffee.

"Sorry," he said. "Hey, Jake asked me and Samson to lunch," he lowered his voice.

"When?" she asked, her hand sweating against the coffee cup.

"Today, and a couple of the editors from down the hall, too." He stopped talking.

"What do you think it means?" she asked.

"I don't know, but it makes it hard to work."

"It'll work out all right, Victor," she filled in his silences. "It's just hard waiting."

"Well, anyway," he said, resuming his normal tone. "Listen to this: The AP says the prisons are filled with guys who can't stand having anyone within twenty feet of them. That's more space than the four of us have each got in our own apartment, by the way. They got so crowded, the wire says, that they killed. Crimes of passion, Sonya!" He sounded excited. "What I mean," he became cool, calculated, "is that at home it's packed with an army of children and here I'm surrounded by twenty guys eating the same Danish. I want space, at least an office of my own." He made some chewing sounds.

"Last week you said you'd pace out the children's room to see how it could be subdivided," she replied, knowing he was now working up to his favorite topic.

"Two more years and we'd have to move anyway, private schools, so forth, so listen to this: Four bedrooms, brook, eight acres, Greenwich . . ."

"Greenwich is where wives become matrons," she responded rapidly, interrupting the details of the ad.

He stopped reading the ad. "They can do it in Manhattan too," he pointed out.

They were both silent.

"What are you doing?" he asked.

"Trying to get out of here by ten thirty." The grocery list was sitting by the telephone. She wrote down *liver paté* and *garlic*.

"Where are you going?"

"Where I go every day, the playground." She heard the Schrafft's wagon bell announce a final choice of Danish.

"Sonya, try to get some rest today. You're working too hard."

"Sure," she said, looking at the clock.

"Okay," he answered. "I'll see you later." They hung up.

Livi was crying. She needed to be changed. Sonya carried her to the changing table and undid her diaper, replaced it with dry, emptied the diaper in the toilet, set it on Livi's side of the sink. In the bedroom Peter stood transfixed while Captain Kangaroo solemnly interviewed a guest attired as an alligator. She removed a sopping diaper from Peter and put on a clean one.

Sonya decided not to finish rinsing the pile of diapers in the bathroom sink. They'd have to wait if she were going to get the babies to the park. Damn, the grocery list. Full speed ahead, the cold wash. Back in the kitchen, she set a cold wash of her own blouses and slacks into the washer and picked up her grocery list. What would Victor like? Her brains had vanished like old dandelions, their fancy fluffing about in her cranial cavity would neatly fulfill her complete feminization, at least in her father's terms. Peter ran in and climbed on her, reaching for her pencil, crumpling her paper.

"Don't climb on me now, Peter," she said, setting him down. He started up again. "Don't," she said too harshly, suddenly shouting. That never worked. Peter lay on the floor and pressed his face to the linoleum, sobbing. She had no luck comforting him. Outdoors. They had to get out. She dialed the grocery store think-

ing that something snackable might come to mind as
she waited to give her order, but there was no delay at
the market and the clerk was speedy. She had to rattle
off her list without pause or mention of snacks in the
vortex of sobs.

Peter hammered the floor with his plastic hammer
while Sonya made a bottle for Olivia, filled a thermos
with apple juice, wrapped the bottle in newspaper, went
to the bathroom, found a few extra diapers, managed
to locate her nail polish and nail file, and threw all the
things into a shoulder bag. She lifted the bag and Olivia
and shooed Peter out the door, shutting it and catching
his hand before he started down the stairs. At the bottom of the three, slowly descended flights, Sonya put
Livi in the carriage stored behind the stairs and
fastened down the little seat that held Peter atop the
carriage.

It was bright outdoors, getting hot. Sonya turned
toward the heavy green foliage at the end of the street
and sailed the carriage over the curb successfully, not
having to rear back and head over a second time. Across
Riverside the sidewalk was level, no curbs to go up and
down. Smooth sailing to the park entrance. Sonya felt
the pressure of the morning fall away as she moved
past trucks and cars whose sounds required no action
from her, truck drivers who were not about to ask her
to change a tire.

A small wind was blowing the leaves in the trees
and there were even birds singing. Aunt Monica must

have enjoyed these sounds at her leisure, walking free, not attached to a vehicle that hauled two children, just her own knee muscles concentrating on lifting her own feet.

While Monica had forsaken marriage for the violin, Sonya's mother had given up the cello for a soldier. The last picture of the two girls taken before their paths diverged appeared on a Christmas card of long ago, where Sonya's mother spread her knees around her instrument and stared straight out at the viewers while Monica turned her bony profile to the world and stuck her violin beneath her chin. That spring vacation Sonya's mother had met her soldier and the sisters parted ways. Throughout their twenties each stubbornly maintained that *she* had made the right choice, but thereafter, rather hesitantly, suggested that the other had. And Monica had walked alone down Riverside while everybody's nineteenth century of the mind had turned into the twentieth, and while her own thirties turned into the forties that carried her out of the childbearing years. Sonya, who had hoped to raise her children without lowering herself, arrived in the playground, lifted Peter off the carriage seat and stretched the mosquito net over Livi.

She handed Peter a wooden locomotive which he clutched possessively to his chest, screaming, "Mine! Mine!" at the slightest lurch in his direction. Olivia woke. Sonya unscrewed the cup on Peter's thermos of apple juice. She unwrapped the bottle of milk and picked up Livi. Peter appeared, magically, pulling at her ankles. "You climb up, Peter, sit by me." She could not give him a hand.

"You carry me," he answered.

"I can't now, you climb."

"Carry me!" he cried.

"Here, take my hand." She tucked the bottle under her chin to free her right hand. He got up and begged for juice. Reaching behind her, she grasped the unscrewed cap and poured the juice one-handed. When the baby was unguarded, Peter lunged at her and Sonya pressed Livi to her left shoulder, but gently so as not to hurt her neck. She leaned with the right half of her body against Peter, but gradually so as not to knock him off the bench. She held back the scream of pain when he pinched a bit of her thigh under his new saddle shoes and his thirty pounds of weight. She did nicely, but she failed to keep from spilling the newly poured juice over herself and the bench. One of the nicest things about the playground was that nothing spilled had to be wiped up.

She poured more juice and Peter drank it, reassured.

"He's getting over it," the pucci-scarfed woman said when Peter walked off to the sandbox with his locomotive. "But he'll get jealous again when she starts to walk."

Sonya laid Livi back in the carriage, replacing the net that protected her from yellowjackets and curious children. She talked and filed and polished her nails and sat luxuriously in the sun. Peter was playing with a boy named Tom, and with Tom's truck.

She had two nails painted when Peter screamed as Tom walked off with his truck. Sonya put the cap back on the nail polish and jumped up. Peter threw his arms around her knees and sobbed.

"Come on," she said, "let's look for stones." She sat down beside him at the base of a tree.

"Here's one stone," he said. "And here's another stone." What a miracle, he could talk.

"And here's a rock, Mummy," he said, handing her a bigger stone. He could tell stones from rocks, and her from other women.

"May I have the rock back, Mummy?" They played pass the rock. She looked down and saw that only two of her fingernails were painted. They shone and reflected light off their hard, white surfaces. Very pretty, very nice.

"Here," she said, "here's one stone. And here's another stone. That is two stones. You have two stones in your hand." You did so well on words, let's do numbers now.

When Tom came back to dig beside Peter, Sonya slipped away. The sun was hot on the newly painted blue bench. She wanted very much to stretch out and go to sleep. She would wake up if Peter needed her, or Livi. But would it look funny and, though she didn't mind looking funny, was it fair to make Peter live the

life of the kid whose Mum slept on park benches? Her
head nodded, she was edging into sleep. Maybe she
could sleep sitting up. She let her eyelids droop, but
respectably so, and her vision was narrowed to the
sandbox, each set of hands practicing some law of the
universe she remembered vaguely from the science
text she had once worked on, long before. The little
girl's hands doing displacement, transfer of mass, moving sand from one location to another. The boy's filling
up an empty basket, putting dense mass, sand, where
formerly there was only sparse mass, air. Another set
of hands pouring, eyes watching the grains fall in the
classic pattern, thinning at the edges as the sand is
pulled earthward from the uptilted pail. Another pair of
hands throws sand wildly in the air. Now it falls, gracefully, innocently, uninterrupted even when it lands in
the eyes of a neighbor, it is innocent, following an innocent course.

The noon whistle blew. Time to get back. She
could nap when the children did. First she would have
to go to Broadway for the dry cleaning. She found Peter
and picked him up and set him in the carriage seat and
started up the hill. Steep, hard going, she must be
pushing forty-five pounds. Ah, the inclined plane. At
least God had paved it for her.

Sonya came up out of sleep through death, bones, de-
cay, stones. If stones could feel would they have a sense

of slowness? Or does it not seem slow inside something slow? That is, does a fruit fly know how fast it lives? That it will be dead before dark?

"HelLO," Sonya answered at the bedside extension.

"You didn't get any rest?" Victor asked.

"You just woke me up."

"Somebody's always sleeping there. I can't read your brain waves from here. Hey," he spoke faster, "Jake sat me next to him at lunch. Nothing specific, but I've got the feeling it's affirmative, maybe by September."

"Terrific." She was now too tired to exude. "I'm glad." He'd said the same thing the week before.

He was silent for a minute. "I'm researching the sewer project at 79th and Riverside. Our neighbors are on the rampage."

"Oh," she replied, "I think I saw a poster on it." What had it said? She had forgotten.

"Well, what did you do today?" He sounded peeved.

"Nothing." It was out before she could stop it. She knew what was coming next.

"What else?" There was never enough for Victor.

"Stuff." How did one describe it? Did he want to hear about how she let the diapers wait?

"Did you develop the pictures from the weekend?" Victor asked.

"No, I did not develop the pictures from the weekend." She had let her voice get too precise but what could his vision of her life and times be?

"Never mind me then, Sonya. Just ignore me completely, tend to the children." He hung up, angrily. She decided not to call back but before she could lie down the phone rang again. Victor's younger sister.

"Never mind marriage," Sonya said to Virginia. "So what if he doesn't call? Stay single, go out to dinner, buy pretty clothes, get your hair done, see a movie, read *The New York Times,* remain a more interesting person." Sonya sat down on the floor.

"Sonya, stop it! You're supposed to be my example. My analyst keeps telling me, hear what Sonya says, do what Sonya does!"

Sonya lay flat on the floor, taking a long, slow Breath Is Life breath as described in her Yoga book. "A half hour a day," the book began, "can easily be arranged for daily practice."

"Breath is life, Virginia," she said, after a long pause inhaling.

"Sonya, I can't afford to get negative about marriage."

"Marriage isn't life, Virginia," she said slowly, on the exhale.

"Sonya, cut it out! I've got to have a positive influence."

"Breath is life, Virginia," she repeated after another inhale and her voice sounded tinny, backed by too much air.

Virginia whispered that her boss had come around the door of her office and she hung up. Sonya climbed back onto the bed, her head was heavy, her eyelids dropping. The phone rang. She slipped back down to the floor, crossed her right ankle over her left thigh in a semi-lotus and picked up the receiver.

"Sonya?" It was her office calling. "Can you shoot fish?"

"I usually try not to," she rubbed her eyes. "And I always beg the man I'm with to take out the hook."

"Sonya, you just subway down to the aquarium and shoot some fish but don't let the glass reflect. Any fish. It's about how fish don't get tired. Water, their bodies, they don't fight gravity all the time. Researchers think maybe they don't even die, Sonya!"

"Harold, I'm trying to take a nap." She tried to lift her left foot into place on her right thigh.

"Sonya, don't you understand? Just a little project. Maybe ten hours in all." Harold sounded rushed.

"That's the trouble with it, Harold, ten hours isn't steady. I have to have steady. I can't work without a babysitter and I can't hire a sitter without work." She tried to speak slowly, but pleasantly, like a TV announcer. "Ten hours of agency babysitting would be a hundred dollars—if you count their cabs and their four-hour minimum. And besides, my son is in no shape for a stranger. The fish, Harold, let them eat cake."

"Okay, okay." Harold sighed. "But I thought you wanted work?"

"Sleep, Harold, I want sleep."

She unfolded onto the rug again, flattening herself to the floor. Her eyes shut. The doorbell rang. A man delivered her groceries. She paid him but had only fifteen cents left in her purse for a tip. She fetched him another twenty cents from her private dime bank and started to put the groceries away. The kitchen was too small. If only Victor would put up a shelf. The terrible monologue had begun. On the great record player of the mind, the afternoon disc began to spin, the voice to sing: "I am innocent, dum de da, I am innocent, la la."

Popsicle goo had leaked onto the floor from the corner of the box. Too messy to leave for the cleaning woman, she judged with a part of her mind not busily singing while with another section of cortex she caused her hands to reach for paper towels. It was dull, this round of tasks, but an inventive woman could live happily with this routine. It must be easier than working in a subway change booth. A calm, reasonable woman could walk about the house immaculately dressed and with her nails done. A woman like that would perform her posture exercises while unpacking the groceries and cream her hands while the bottles sterilized. Such a woman, her price outshining rubies, would arise before the babies and accomplish her toilet in the magnificent light of dawn. Such a one would anoint her body with Jean Naté while humming the Magnificat. Such-a-One would open and close doors silently and neatly, she would plump up pillowcases the full five recommended times and her shoebag would not be ripped. Most assuredly, it would not smell of old shoes. Such-a-One walked smoothly like a melody, lightening the household and causing it to reverberate with the music of the spheres—indeed, tap a crystal glass in her kitchen cupboard and the distant toilet seat would sing back a resounding, rebounding, echoing note, indicating how clean, happy, and carefree it was. Such-a-One, Such-a-One, even her name was somehow heavenly. Could she be related to Big Boy? That golden, chubby fellow with the laughing, yes, laughing curls? Sonya dropped a ripe tomato in front of the refrigerator and it splattered, dampening her big toe and staining her new sandals. She could hear Peter talking in his crib. It was three thirty P.N., post nap, the hard part of the day. "But I am innocent," the record insisted, "innocent."

Peter was grumpy on waking, more than he had been before Olivia's birth. Poor Peter, would he soon be reduced to biting Olivia's fingers or dropping her into the toilet bowl, tactics practiced upon younger siblings by children from her own playground? She coaxed him out of bed and into clean diapers.

Could she keep her eyes open and not stare glassily into space? Staring was bad for Peter. Maybe if she freshened up, changed her clothes. Her clothes. She had never hung the cool wash and by now her blouses would be dry and wrinkled. After she opened the washer and bent to separate Victor's socks from her underpants and Peter's pajama bottoms from Olivia's nightshirts, Peter opened his pan drawer (Spock, page X, provide a pan drawer in the kitchen for the toddler) and took out two pots and hit them together like a drum, making a thwack that woke up the baby.

"AAAH!" Livi cried from her cradle ready to eat, but Sonya was trying to teach her to increase her stomach capacity by giving her larger, more distantly spaced meals. It sounded as if Olivia could be held off only by being taken outdoors. Sonya shut the door of the washer and quickly packed up food and toys for the park.

The atmosphere of the playground in the afternoon was different from that of the morning. Women were there on larks or out of desperation, not as a matter of course. With Sonya the trip had begun as desperation but somehow the aura of the park managed to provide an antidote and Peter, who at first sat on Sonya's lap or stood leaning nearby, eventually went off to swing on the jungle gym with small gestures of bravado, holding tight to the bar, lifting his feet a little off the ground and carefully bending his knees to bring them up, swinging in an arc of several inches and looking discreetly proud.

Olivia watched the shadows of leaves playing on the white wall of her carriage and kicked at the mosquito net that hung low over her feet until they got stuck in it and the net became a constant presence, a friend. OOOH, OOOH she said. OOOH was for happiness, French, debonaire, with lips pursed forward and the beginning of a smile. AAAH was despair, with lips pulled back and tongue trembling.

Sonya used the free time to examine herself. Her shirt smelled of vomit on the left shoulder and urine on the midriff; her sandals were stained with tomato juice, her pink slacks were sticky and smudged. Was this post-partum depression? Such-a-One would blush and turn away.

Sonya jumped up to rescue Peter from a seesaw and grazed the board, pressing a splinter into her hand. Mummy-of-Afflictions, why do I offer up my flesh? She helped Peter walk along the board. Such-a-One is beautiful and black, gliding through the jungle in a clean flowered sari with four or five clean-clothed little folk running behind her. They do not clutch at *her* dress with sticky hands, she does not let them muss her hair. A drum calls among the trees: "Come home to supper Such-a-One, the men are back from the military, the pots simmering on the fire require your knowing hand to measure flavor and produce A*R*O*M*A." Sonya picked out the splinter and then she returned to the bench to feed Olivia.

Sonya dreaded leaving the park. She chatted with benchmates. This was the day's last stretch of sanity. In the playground in the company of other mothers, she felt she could cope as well as any of them. But once home, where she was not the master, she lost her sense of capability. There were still a good number of women around, it couldn't be too late. Peter complained of hunger and she fed him cheese and crackers and juice. She finally asked the time, almost seven! She had been fooled by the presence of women who had come back into the playground after supper. She picked up Peter.

"Come on, it's late. Daddy is home. Daddy is hungry." She set him on the seat atop the carriage and strapped him there against his will, the carriage careened, and she caught a right hook to her hip. She pushed the carriage out of the park with Peter scream-ing on top and Olivia emitting faint "Aaahs" from be-neath Peter's seat, where she spent her riding time in the dark, cramped quarters of the second child. At the first curb, Sonya went over too fast and nearly lost the whole cartload of dump truck, sand pail, son, and daughter. "I am innocent," the voice repeated, soaring into an intricate madrigal.

"Where have you been?" Victor asked when he opened the door for them, beer can in hand. He did not seem too angry.

"At the playground." While Victor greeted the children, Sonya unpacked the outdoor bag.

"What's to snack?" Victor asked at the kitchen

doorway, not too attractive in his Norwegian net shirt that showed off his tan as well as a bit of belly.

"Liver paté."

"I thought you ordered groceries today."

"I did."

"We had liver paté last week."

"Would you please change the light bulb in the bathroom?"

"Snappy! Snappy!" Victor grimaced and moved back into the bedroom to rejoin the television.

Sonya set milk on the counter for Peter and undressed Olivia. She ran water in a plastic tub and balanced it on her clotheswasher, and plumped Olivia into the bath, keeping her own left hand dry and unslippery behind Olivia's back. Olivia folded up into a fetal-like position when she felt the water and she smiled. Did she remember the watery land? Olivia continued to produce her contagious smile and Sonya, holding her with one hand, sprinkling liquid germ-killer soap over her knees with the other, smiled at her daughter. Olivia was her joy now; like an Italian mother she took her daughter to herself, was always stroking her neck, enclosing her soft, vulnerable bones, in moments she stole from the day's demands.

"More milk!" Peter banged his cup behind her.

"Ask Daddy to get it for you, please," Sonya said, unable to free a hand.

"More milk Daddy!" He banged his cup louder.

"Victor?" Sonya called. It was only a three and a half room apartment!

"MORE MILK!"

"Victor!" Sonya shouted. Olivia was slipping into the water.

"What is it?" Victor answered quietly from the bedroom.

"Can you get Peter more milk?" Sonya continued shouting, Olivia continued slipping.

No answer came.

With her toe Sonya picked up the towel that had fallen, flipped it to her right hand, stuck it between her front teeth where it hung down in front of her chest, lifted Olivia from the bath, pressed her wet body against the draped towel, switched arms rapidly and captured both towel and daughter as they slid downwards, chucked the wrapped Olivia under one arm, removed the top of a milk bottle with her free hand and poured another glass for Peter.

"Sonya?" Victor queried as he made his way to the door of the bedroom. "What were you calling me for?" He glared as she crossed the hallway with the wet baby.

"Nothing," she said sweetly over her shoulder.

"Nothing! What the hell did you get me out here for?"

"Spite." She smiled.

"Shit." Victor swung back to the television.

Sonya buttoned Olivia's nightgown and laid her

in the crib, recrossed the hallway to Peter, who was still drinking milk, recrossed to the bathroom to rinse diapers. Stretch type in Peter's pail, smooth type in Olivia's. The stains in the diapers hardly showed in the dim light available in the bathroom. Victor, unlike his own father, was willing to help with the children but his willingness was whimsical and appropriate to his mood rather than to the demands of the situation. Furthermore, there appeared to be a magic formula for effective request, a formula she had not yet grasped.

She walked into the bedroom, selected the exact center of it, stood quietly and said distinctly, "Will you please bathe Peter?"

"Sure thing," Victor said, rising from the sagging chair, slapping her on the thigh. "I, Victor, will take over. Always glad to help out with the little folks."

That was the secret, stand in the exact center of the room.

"And I'll make you a drink," he said, "with maybe a little liver paté." His curly hair was so long now it ran almost to the band of his awful net shirt. What had changed his mood? She didn't know. Cause and effect had come unglued, she floated as the prey of whimsy, as children lived.

"I spilled my milk on purpose!" Peter called from the kitchen.

Victor never returned with the drink. He whisked Peter into the bathroom, ran the water hard, threw in a cup of bubble bath, lifted his son over the side—

"NO! I don't want to get in!" Peter screamed, kicking his way back to the floor and running out the door.

Sonya took that opportunity to go to the bathroom herself, barely making it up off the toilet seat before Peter pushed the door open again.

In her crib Olivia fussed. Sonya jounced her mattress and played with her, until she cracked an elbow painfully against the railing of the crib. Aaah, she thought, Aaah. The physical life is not for me. Livi quieted down and began to watch her mobiles.

The frying pan was in back of all the other pans. Impatiently, Sonya smashed the whole bunch of pans to the floor, grabbed for the big one. The noise made Olivia cry the sort of wail that would continue until stopped by a haphazard pat on the back, a cry governed by the second law of physics or was it the first? Or wasn't it even physics? Information no longer had importance, only action, only getting through to the ultimate goal, which was lying down. She left the pan on the floor, went into the children's room and delivered the magical pat. When she once again knelt by the fallen pan she noticed that Someone, Blessed-Be-She, had put it away with egg caked along the sides. She scrubbed it.

The doorbell rang. The super had come back to fix the slow leak in the toilet.

"All clear," she said, ushering him into the bathroom littered with soaked towels and Peter's clothes.

Hurriedly, she wiped up the floor, slapped the bath-towels over the tub, pulled the tub drain open, replaced her fallen film developing box to the corner of the tub, and rescued the soap.

"Cut it out!" In the children's room, Victor slapped Peter and Peter screamed. Olivia screamed. Sonya rescued Olivia from the hubbub in the children's room and moved her to the cradle in the living room, rocked her a minute and returned to the kitchen. Where was the corkscrew?

"Sonya!" Victor came in, whispering. "I can't take it any longer, will you finish him? I'll make you a drink."

"It's a bargain," she said. Why didn't she dare say no? "Will you open the wine?" She knew he wouldn't be able to find the corkscrew either.

On her way to the children's room, she was way-laid by the super, who asked her for his money.

"Victor," she whispered, returning to the kitchen, "We've got to tip the super."

"You do it," he said, mixing drinks.

"I ran out of money," she said.

"What about the ten I just gave you?" He looked startled.

"I spent it."

"Spent it!" A look of disbelief crossed his face. He stopped stirring ice and went for his wallet.

"Time to read, Peter," she said as she walked to his crib and swept him up before he could protest.

She settled in the rocker with a book and him on her lap.

"What is that?" he asked, pointing at a fire engine.

"That's a fire engine."

"No," he said, "it isn't. It's a truck."

"You like to think it's a truck," she said (X, page X—she could no longer remember who had said what).

"IT'S A TRUCK!" he screamed. She slowly turned the pages to the end of the book.

"Put your head down now," she stretched him out in the crib but he regained his feet instantly.

"I want juice! I want juice!"

She brought juice. He tried to spill it. She hung on.

"I want Daddy!" Victor came in for a kiss. Peter flung his arms around his neck and tried to climb out but Victor moved away. He left Peter with one leg over the crib rail.

"I can't rock him tonight," Victor sighed in the hallway when the cries did not subside. "A man deserves a little leisure," he said, reaching into the kitchen for his glass.

Lacking rights of refusal, Sonya rocked Peter in the darkened room and sang while his body grew heavier and he sank against her shoulder. What would have happened if she had refused? As she rocked, she fought against the sleep that had hovered about her all day. Finally Peter breathed heavily and she laid him down in the crib.

. . .

The bottom of Sonya's right heel was tender to step on; she raised it off the floor as she stood cooking in the bright, hot kitchen. She sliced the scallions and put the steak in the hot pan. She dropped the frozen beans into the bubbling water and slipped the cover over them. She set the timer. Another few minutes and she could sit down.

She turned the steak, lowered the bean flame, and then set the table in the hallway with silverware, glasses, and candles and turned out the overhead light. The table looked appealing but the combined presence of playpen, desk, table, and chairs in the small central hallway took away all sense of repose. The timer pinged and she returned to the kitchen to lift the seared steak from the pan, made the butter and scallion sauce, drained the beans, and brought the two plates to the table. She touched a match to the candlewicks and called Victor from his chair.

She sat, falling heavily onto the straight-back rattan chair. Oh, she was still wearing the urine-marked shirt and the dirt-smudged slacks. After dinner she would shower and change.

"At last," Victor said, stretching as he pushed himself out of the armchair, "I'm starved." His belly was beginning to bulge over his jeans.

"Tell me again what Jake said," Sonya asked. She felt her body relax at the prospect of stillness, food, and drink. She wanted to end the feeling of argument that lingered from the phone conversation.

"First, he took us to lunch, steak with asparagus tips and French tarts." He looked pleased remembering.

So he had eaten steak for lunch! Sonya felt inexplicably beaten.

" 'You sit here,' he said to me, pointing to his right." Victor re-enacted the scene with his muscular forearm. "That was sort of the peak, though. There wasn't anything he said, just a tone of treating me with curiosity, like he'd be working with me soon and wanted to get to know my strengths and weaknesses." Victor was halfway through his steak.

"Who sat on his left?" she asked, straining for something to say, her mind gone blank. The food tasted very good, had she eaten lunch? She could not remember.

"Some guy down the hall, bald." Victor reported bits of conversation as he cut into the last steak on his plate and finished up his beans. Sonya eyed them as they vanished; she kept on eating.

"It was hard in the afternoon, though. For the first time Samson and I didn't joke about Jake." Then he finished eating and raised his hands triumphantly above his head. "Say, how about a little more steak and beans for a hard-working fella, huh?" He indicated his empty plate.

"Would you mind getting them yourself? I'm not ready." Sonya cut into her steak.

"I'll wait, I don't mind waiting. A fella enjoys resting after the strains of the day, and then he likes a little attention in light of the fact that he's knocked his brains all day to bring home the cash to send the kids to college." He looked genuinely pleased. He leaned onto the back legs of his chair.

Sonya cut slowly into her steak. She didn't believe that Victor really wanted to be a producer. He used to say he felt trapped by it.

"Sure you don't want to be on camera instead?" she asked as she cut into her steak.

"Too chancy. Producing's safe." He balanced on the legs precariously.

Sonya chewed deliberately. Safe! She'd married Victor for everything else!

"I have to figure the odds, Sonya. This way I'll make enough to save two or three thousand a year and we can . . ."

Sonya jumped up and grabbed his plate and hurried into the kitchen.

"Buy a house in the suburbs," he called in as she lifted the lid of the bean pot and burned her hand on the steam. "What do you think?" he directed his voice into the kitchen.

"What about your ski area?" she called back.

"Be realistic, Sonya," he sighed.

"I've already said," she answered calmly as she returned with the plates, "that if we use a little imagination we could subdivide the children's room, build in sleeping lofts, furnish it with rolled-up sorts of Japanese things, and get by very nicely." She set his plate down in front of him.

"That's not so practical. They each need a real room." He returned to an upright position and started on his second plate of steak.

"Or if we took a long time looking, we could find a bigger apartment in the city." She ate a single bean, stalling for time.

"I've been looking for two years, Sonya. Rents are five times what we pay. Now if your aunt had thought to leave us three bedrooms . . ." he belched.

Tears collected in Sonya's eyes. She had a feeling this might turn out to have been their final talk on moving. "I don't want to leave," she said, quietly. "A yard would turn my life into my mother's."

"Come on," he said, "what about freedom for the kids and for you, too? They're never out of your sight at that playground." Victor dipped beans in steak juice. "It would be a hell of a lot easier on you, Sonya. You could just shoo the kids out the back door and drink coffee."

"The playground is the best part of the day," she answered. She realized that her arguments were as meaningless as his; it was a matter of will and something had happened to hers. The tears reached the rims of her eyes. Her mother had made a habit of tearing up at the supper table, nothing infuriated Sonya more. And how like him to suggest there were hours for coffee.

"Now don't cry, Sonya," Victor poured more wine in her glass. "We don't have to go if you don't want to. But look at Rose Kennedy. She never complained." He moved his chair to hers, started to put his arm around her.

"Oh, I don't complain, Victor. I have not yet begun to complain. You know it is not in my nature to complain," the words came out rigidly spaced. Sonya drained the giant glass of wine.

"Listen, Sonya," he said, encircling her shoulders, "I don't want to go either. I'd really rather have a ski resort, remember?"

"You don't want a ski resort," she said, coldly. "And neither do I." Rolling up her napkin, she was careful not to blink so that the tears would not show up on her cheeks.

"What do you want, then?" he shouted, suddenly dropping his arm, standing above her, leaning threateningly over her. "I'll tell you what I don't want," he continued, without pausing for her answer. "I don't want to type up amusing pieces on Santa Clauses whose beards get caught in subway turnstiles! Not any more! Nor do I care to sit stuffed behind sliding doors, saying 'yessir' to the boss and 'step lively' to the underlings —working up heart muscle for a cardiac." His tone switched from anger to amusement, back and forth. Was he trying to avoid a real fight?

"You can't have everything you want, Sonya," he explained patronizingly. "So tell me, give me one reasonable little request of yours. Tell me one sane, rational thing you want from me." He leaned forward expectantly.

"I would like you to help me with the dishes," she replied, calmly, suddenly finding the world clarified. She looked up from her plate.

"Oh you would, would you?" he shouted. "Well, I don't feel like it!"

"Nor do I," she replied, but Victor did not hear as he made his way to the living room, enraged, to stretch out on the couch at right angles to the sleeping baby.

Sonya stood up for the last time, she hoped, before bed. She carried the dishes into the kitchen and ran hot soapy water over them, deciding to let them soak all night. She reached up for a paper towel to dry her hands and knocked the loose roll into the sink. She crossed the hallway to the linen closet, but when she opened the door to reveal the haphazard linens, she simply pressed her damp hands against a pile of towels and continued on her way across the hallway into her bedroom. She lay down without washing her face or inserting her diaphragm. Only another few weeks and her doctor would give her back her coil. Her eyes shut.

"Sonya," Victor whispered in her ear, no longer angry. "When do we have supper?"

"Are you trying to say you're still hungry?" she asked, almost asleep.

"Yes."

"You can look in the refrigerator, I'm very tired. And would you please turn out the kitchen light, I forgot."

"Okay, you rest." Victor swung up and crossed the hallway to the kitchen. She heard him step over the threshold.

"For Pete's sake, Sonya!" he shouted. "You promised not to leave dishes in the sink! The cockroaches!"

"Oh," she called, raising her head from the pillow. "You do them."

"Why the hell should I?" he shouted back. "I'm not in charge of the house!"

"You'll wake the kids," she said quietly into the mattress beneath the pillow, her open eye focused on the two polished and three unpolished nails of her left hand.

"And why don't you ever have anything to eat around here? There's no snacks. When do you order?"

"I told you I ordered today," she said inaudibly into the mattress. She should have made more fuss about his sitting next to Jake. Tomorrow.

"Sonya, please get me some decent snacks when you order." He snapped off the kitchen light and stomped into the bathroom and slammed the door.

Olivia cried and Sonya got up. When she swallowed, her throat felt scratchy.

"Very well, then, go feed the baby!" He got into bed as she was getting out. He pulled up the sheet, glad to avoid her for another evening. Things hadn't been so good lately, even though she'd finally stopped nursing.

Sonya warmed Olivia's bottle and fed her in the dark living room. She rocked as she held the bottle to Livi's lips, her mind flitted about for images of peace: she noticed the faces of wicker kings from a distant island society that peopled her hot living room without benefit of Polynesian breezes. Eastward, toward morning from Polynesia, there was a Japanese tea table with women in flowered kimonos ironed neatly (when, Oh, Such-a-One, when?) and with the open sleeves moving gracefully in silken patterns as the fleshy arm that seemed to have no bones within poured the tea just so, and slowly, each movement done slowly and gracefully. That was the answer, slowness. The forced slow motion of the tea ceremony must have been invented by the most desperate women in the world. Walking slowly and gracefully, the toe, the ball of the foot, the arch, the heel, Sonya passed through the clutter in the hallway to the children's room and laid Olivia in her crib. She glided back to the refrigerator with the dirty bottle. There she could store it all night without washing it. Slowly, in her new floating gait, she turned back and bumped into the clotheswasher. What had become of the cool wash? She raised the lid of the washer. Her blouses and slacks were still intertwined with each other, wrinkled dry. She shut the lid, turned out the light, and groped her way back to the bed where Victor slept.

The Goddess of the Baby Park

Sonya took her seat on the playground's white, middle-class, thirties, second child, part-time-employed bench, even though she hadn't handled a free-lance assignment in months. Would they retire her from that bench if she didn't take a free-lance assignment soon? She settled down between the geriatric nurse and the remedial reading teacher. The geriatric nurse had two daughters, the teacher now had two sons. Sonya imagined both women in bed with their husbands. Was the two-daughtered nurse's husband given to premature ejaculation, sending his sperm into acid vaginal waters where the short-lived male-carrying cells died before reaching safety? Or was it that the nurse was cold—never coming to an orgasm that would release a base solution where the faster male-carrying cells could outdistance the slow but longer-lived female carriers? Or did strong women breed strong daughters by the power of suggestion?

The teacher was wearing make-up—a sure sign that her second son was sitting up unaided, that things were getting back to normal. The nurse still looked bad. Her second daughter was lying flat in an infant's suit and the nurse had stuffed her uncombed hair into a kerchief and her unmoisturized, uncolored face showed lines around the mouth.

At this time of year life was on its way out, going from green to brown in what would be the final journey for millions of individual leaves and insects, ladybugs, and old peach pits. Mum N seemed to be putting out a last show of fertility, a nervous show that saw leaves as too green, trees as too leafy, and grass too tall and wild, the smell too close to garbage. Sonya wanted iced tea very badly but she settled for a popsicle and sucked at the purple ice while Peter drew the moisture from his pink one. The pregnant English professor tied her fuzzy dog at the gate of the playground and wheeled her son inside.

"It satisfies their sucking instinct," the remedial teacher said, indicating the children holding popsicles.

Sonya looked down and continued to suck, listening to the talk around her.

"It's all set," the nurse said to the approaching English professor while stroking the head of her girl.

"Hal says he can bring the cradle over any time. But the baby swing and the playpen will have to wait a while," she nodded toward the carriage where her baby lay.

"Terrific," the English professor answered, adjusting a blue-striped maternity blouse as she sat down. "That's terrific. I'm going to keep the cradle at my mother's in Jersey."

"We're wondering how soon we can give you the cradle," the nurse proceeded cautiously. "I mean, it's in our front hallway, we couldn't fit it under the bed." She paused and opened a pretzel bag for the girl at her knee.

"Oh," the English professor answered. "Well, sure." She opened a Cheez-It bag for her son. "I guess we can keep it in our hallway for a few months. My mother wouldn't take it now. How about Sunday?"

"Terrific," the nurse replied, biting into a pretzel. "Around two?"

"Terrific." The English professor finished the conversation and looked sadly away.

"Stopping at two?" Sonya inquired of the nurse, while beginning to perform her vagina-tightening exercises.

"Yes," the nurse answered. "It'd be great to have a boy but we'd have to move out of the city." She shrugged.

"I can't quite decide to stop," Sonya said. She pushed her hair behind her ears and, looking straight

ahead, tightened urethra, vagina, and rectum in the
order the book prescribed. In an earlier century she
could have left the decision to chance. She tightened
her stomach muscles next but not much happened.
"No stomach muscles at all!" the dance instructor had
scolded at the introductory lesson the day before.

"You can't have more than two," the remedial
teacher interrupted, leaning forward. "Population explosion. You've got to adopt and you've got to adopt
black and you can't adopt just one black so you have
to adopt two and that makes four children and then
you have to move to Montana." She slumped, back
against the bench.

"You have to move with two, anyway," the professor said. "We've got to buy the co-op upstairs or get
out."

Sonya tried her stomach muscles again but nothing doing. She went back to the urethra, vagina, rectum
sequence. There was some life there. Maybe the other
women on the bench were doing theirs, too. All of them
together combating muscle laxity in a great benchline
front.

"And how can we buy a co-op?" the professor continued. "My whole salary goes to child care and cleaning."

"That's why I'm not going back yet," the teacher
remarked from her slumped position. "George says we
clear more money when I'm home."

"I had to go when I did," the English professor

retorted. "Another year at the bottom of the priorities list, eating the broken toast and drinking grapefruit juice when there wasn't enough for more than two glasses of orange and I couldn't have moved."

"But what about your kids?" the teacher responded.

"My son doesn't need me as bad as that," the professor replied, indicating with a small nod the figure of Pauline approaching across the playground with her children and her thermos of Scotch.

Nicole entered the park, pushing Alexandra at a fast clip. Clip. Clipsie. Nicole and Sonya had early determined their different phonic backgrounds—Sonya made her baby diminutives on the *k*-line, that is, Peter, Pee-kee, while Nicole did them on *s*, as in Peter, Pete-sy.

"Sonya!" Nicole was waving as she pushed her stroller faster across the playground. "I telephoned you earlier but your line was busy. I've got to run, due to see him again at ten. Can you watch Alexandra?" They reached the bench.

"Sure," Sonya juggled her morning plans. "Be back by noon?"

"Yes, all her stuff is in the stroller," Nicole hugged the straw-haired girl. "You stay with Peter and Sonya," she instructed her daughter. "You can rock the baby, I'll be back before lunchtime."

"Wish me luck!" Nicole called back to Sonya as she moved quickly away, running toward the exit gate, her hair flying behind her, her narrow body lithe in a jersey pants suit. Sonya realized she had never seen Nicole in anything but jeans and her husband's old shirts before.

"Mummy," Alexandra said. "Mummy's running." She sat in the stroller and followed her vanishing mother with a confident expression. When Nicole was out of sight, her daughter climbed out of the stroller and stood on tiptoe to peer into the carriage where Olivia lay.

"Baby's sleeping," she said, reaching down into the carriage with a dirty hand, sticking her finger toward the baby's mouth, grazing the eyelids.

"Yes, she's sleeping," Sonya replied, holding Alexandra's hand and directing her fingers away from Olivia's eyes and mouth. "Touch her cheek here," she moved the hand farther from the sensitive areas. "Or her hands."

"Baby's sleeping," Alexandra repeated, her fingertips resting on the baby's wrist, as she rocked the carriage with her stomach.

"Yes, sleeping," Sonya answered and sat down on the bench.

The nurse attached plastic roller skates to the feet of her older girl and stood her up. Sonya remembered the metal skates she had once owned, their leather strap, frayed where it rubbed against the buckle, and a skate key that tasted metallic when she put it in her mouth. There had been a gentle slope in the driveway of her three-story house in Eugene and she had learned to divert her vertical, rolling body from a crash into the garage doors by some fancy footwork that spun her around and started her up the slope again. It had been lovely until the day when her best friend had ceremoniously hung up their skates in the garage, stating emphatically, "We're too old for that now." After that, Sonya had stopped spinning. The nurse's daughter had only gotten plastic, what would she know of life at large?

The little girl struggled with the skates, too young for them, but eager, holding on to her mother's hand. The nurse walked in front of Sonya and all the children who—from babies in strollers drooling teething biscuit crumbs to sophisticated three-year-olds—stared at the apparition. Scrunch, scrunch, the plastic made a light, invalid noise on the cement as the girl slid her feet forward on the cheap wheels.

Alexandra stopped leaning her stomach against the carriage and walked toward the bench, where she leaned, instead, on Sonya's knee and watched the roller skater.

"She's skating," Sonya said. There was a silence all along the bench. In the sandbox Peter looked up to catch the word that described the action.

"Mine," Alexandra murmured, tossing the word out softly on the quiet.

"Would you like a turn on the skates?" Sonya asked.

"Mine," she replied, a bit more forcibly.

"Say, can Alexandra try those when Christina's done?" Sonya asked from the bench and mothers all down the line repeated the request. The skates began to circulate, then split up and become one skate at a time—after one sporting girl had found things too chancy with both feet wheeled.

Sonya snapped a skate onto Alexandra's left foot and Peter took the steps up the sandbox to watch.

Alexandra stood up, holding tight to Sonya's right hand. She hopped and skated, hopped and skated. Boys seated on large-wheeled tricycles paused to watch as various girls attached the smaller wheels directly to their feet but no boys volunteered for that exercise. The girls drew things to their own bodies, whereas the boys remained protective of their integrities.

It got hotter. Popsicles came and went.

Livi woke and Sonya picked her up to hold her. She kissed her neck, remembering Tahitian babies who were never out of touching distance from their mothers and Eskimo women who carried their naked babies strapped to their backs beneath bunched furs. Would each kiss make Livi more trusting and supple in the dance, brave and quick-witted across the Arctic? Or would caresses teach her to draw things to her body, but not to explore, tame, or manage well on an outward quest? Hard to know. Hard to know whether to have a third child, when to go back to work, what moving out meant.

Maybe it would be the best thing for all of them.

Light, air, and for the children schools, freedom, drugs, loneliness, alienation, and unwed pregnancy.

Was she perhaps biased?

Or was her bias her opinion?

Would she see it more clearly later?

Or be brainwashed?

Juice, water, salty pretzels all came into view as the day edged toward noon. Sonya was unwrapping the paper from Alexandra's second popsicle when she caught sight of Nicole returning slowly, steadily covering the ground between the slope outside the gate and the bench where Sonya sat with Alexandra.

"Didn't he like you?" Sonya asked as Nicole dropped her suede purse onto the bench and kissed her daughter.

"He liked me," she replied, reaching for her year-round thermos of hot coffee. "Too much. He just wanted to get me down there to tell me face to face I can have the job. But I don't mean just face to face." She twisted her mouth in a grimace and opened the thermos. The heat still trapped by the insulating walls of the bottle flowed without much impact into the heated air of the playground.

"At least you got it," Sonya encouraged her.

"It's in the bag, so to speak." Nicole lit a cigarette. "Except I'm sort of the bag."

"What's it about?" Sonya dropped her popsicle stick.

"Sex. For a girlie movie, that's not bad." Nicole sipped her coffee.

"Nothing else?" asked Sonya. "No dancing?"

"I'll wiggle my pectorals and that's about it," Nicole sighed.

"Well, it's a start," Sonya felt plain, nobody had asked her to be in a sex movie. Maybe she should put her hair up when she got home.

"I don't know," Nicole leaned forward with her elbows on her knees. "Jerry will be mad, he'll say go ahead, but he'll keep digging me about it."

"What exactly would you do?" Sonya tried to imagine Nicole's naked body. It seemed ordinary, like her own, on the slender side. Alexandra leaned on her mother's jersey-covered thigh.

"It's about a young girl, that's me, who gets into prostitution and some older woman teaches her all about it." Nicole patted Alexandra's back.

"Sounds lesbian," Sonya said, late, beginning to look for Peter's toys. "At least you're the young girl."

"Seventeen, that's me. He disqualified a chick who looked all of fourteen because she had a son." Nicole frowned. "I said I didn't have any children and that I was nineteen. I denied you, Alexandra," she added with an inflection that did not betray her meaning to the girl. She flicked some ashes that caught on the ankle of her flared slacks, juggling cigarette and bag as she fetched out a bubble wand and a bottle of synthetic bubbles.

"You could pass for seventeen," Sonya said, curious to know Nicole's age but politely refraining from the question.

"I'm twenty-four. Lesbian, huh? I forgot to ask if there were lesbian scenes. I don't like that. My friend Agnes had to pretend she was doing it with a goat." Nicole unscrewed the cap of the bubble bottle. "She said he kept pissing all over her."

She blew into the wand and made iridescent bubbles for Alexandra and Peter, who ran over to watch. Other children gathered. The breeze took the bubbles toward the metal fence, the larger ones broke there but the smaller ones got through and up.

"When do you start to shoot?" Sonya fetched Peter's tractor from under the bench and put it on her lap.

"Next week, if I take it." Nicole blew more bubbles. "I'll really have to get in shape if I take it. Hey, what did your instructor say last night?"

"No stomach muscles. No inner thigh muscles, just as you told me. I've been walking wrong for thirty years." Sonya tried to raise her leg with inner instead of outer thigh muscles but nothing lifted. "See? No action."

"At least I know about something, even if it's only muscles," Nicole replied, "that's just what I told you." She switched from blowing through the plastic wand to moving her arm rapidly and gracefully through the air. Many small bubbles resulted.

Sonya caught sight of Nicole's watch. "I've got to get home," she said. "I've got a babysitter coming. Victor got a raise and I'm going to have an afternoon off every week. Today I'm going to take the bus to the Cloisters and sit among the saints." She would sit on an old stone and make a few plans. She turned Olivia on her back so the baby could look up at the trees and strapped Peter on the carriage seat and they were off.

Sonya wheeled out of the playground, but something, a noise in the air into which the bubbles had vanished, caused her to turn her head and look back. There, floating above the playground she saw the huge, faint, billowing shape of a supine female draped in the sky above the baby park. Golden lines sparkled by her head in a kind of Florentine trim and she bucked as she spread her knees above the park while beneath her played forty or fifty children, the baby crop of the last few years, and on the pregnant women's bench sat four whose bellies bloomed out into one of the many semi-circles that embellished the park—from the buttocks of the goddess in the sky to the gentle arcs of the swings that carried little girls higher and higher in a mad rush of the thrill to receive the wind, the fertile wind that blew heart-shaped linden leaves beyond the asphalt of the playground, out through the fence to the earth beyond.

Raking

Victor swallowed, his mouth felt dry. He remembered how sweaty he'd been in the morning, a few minutes before the cameramen had arrived, when the city officials had not yet given in and the rally threatened to begin, small but colorful, perfect. By last-minute magic, things had finally started to mesh under the sound of Victor's voice. Now he triumphantly stuffed papers into his desk, rescuing his pay envelope of three hundred and fifty bucks from the mess. Enough for the rent, the food, the movies. And Sonya, he should take her to dinner, a drink. She needed to get out. He locked the door, his own door at last, and walked to the wide corridor where the girls sat.

There she was, Joan Blumberg, the new researcher. Her knees were smooth under glossy stockings, her flesh illuminated as in Renaissance paintings —a little plump, succulent, not fat.

"Victor," she said coolly, nodding; she had his number. She leaned over the desk toward him so that the low neckline of her dress fell forward giving a view of the top half of her rounded breasts, whose nipples were barely shielded by a bit of flowered cloth.

"Enjoy yourself," he said, suddenly robbed of words. He turned out to the main hall and stood ready to press the DOWN button. Joan was watching him from her desk.

"Oh, I would!" she answered, smiling, her lips widened, the silver shine on them lighter than the pink tongue behind them.

His unsummoned elevator shot to a stop beside him, the door glided open, he entered, smiling at Joan, who waved as the door glided shut. The elevator lowered him smoothly; he remembered Lillian Shamai, his first Christmas dance, a rugless dining room, the same medley over and over. " 'I'm dreaming,' Lillian Shamai, of you," he had whispered in her ear. "Just like I always did before." He swayed in the slow, dark room, perspiring.

"How old are you, Lillian?" he asked quietly.

"Fifteen," she replied even more softly.

"Fifteen! I was sure you were sixteen!"

"Shamai!" his mother had said. "You're Catholic!"

"No TV experience!" the studios had scoffed.

"Marriage!" his father reddened. "Without money!"

"Suburbs!" Well, so what to all of them. He, Victor, would simply forge ahead with a healthy stride, let follow who may. He pushed out of the elevator, walking as fast as the ten men around him, all with wife, kids, a house in the suburbs, memories.

Out the revolving door and he began to run from the dark, slender building which had always seemed to him made fragile and vulnerable by its beauty among the stockier, light-hued skyscrapers that stood like entire nation states, watching one another in their hugenesses across the Balkan valley of Sixth Avenue. He imagined the flags being hoisted atop these fortresses on a day of warfare and the trumpets blaring as the bankers flung themselves down self-operative elevators and out onto Sixth to fight the insurance fellows while the journalists vied at javelins with the hotel operators. He felt jovial by the time he reached the subway entrance and dashed down the first steps only to be slowed by a mass descent into the underworld beneath 50th Street. He tried continually to push thoughts of the unexplored Joan from his mind, as he leaned against the turnstile, as he exited the subway, as he passed a Broadway store front of lost causes—Bobby Kennedy, McCarthy, the Moratorium, even as he climbed the stoop of his brownstone. He ought to think of Sonya; he'd been so hard on her during the summer, worried about getting the job. He inserted the key into the lock, turned it abruptly, and flung open the door. No one home. No sounds. No shapes sleeping on beds. Toys all over the place. He needn't have wasted time worrying that Sonya would become the tight-lipped housewife his mother had been, driving his father off to scrawny broads in Irish bars. Thoughts of Joan in a peaceful ski lodge with fields of virgin snow came to mind; ha, for him that probably meant Sonya in the suburbs—his fantasies being the last faint signal before a move in the opposite direction. Silence. He hung up his suit jacket on top of a blouse of Sonya's; there were no free hangers in the packed closet. He located his rumpled jeans on the back of a chair. No sounds. He turned on the new second-hand hi fi and waited expectantly before he remembered that the tone arm had fallen off the preceding week. Where was his Scotch? His wife? The thousands of children sprung from his loins to defend him from the cameramen's union? He felt abandoned in the empty house. Maybe Sonya and the children were at the playground. He fled.

His feet made a satisfying noise on the stairway, he jogged down the street toward the blur of brown leaves in the park. It would be a great day for a bike ride, but his bicycle had been stolen from the rack in the cellar. How was a fellow to relax in small, perfect Manhattan? Again, Joan.

Fall, the air fresh, the riverside's patch of pseudo-natural landscape beckoned to him. Weren't those squirrels already doing something with their nuts? Ah, nuts, not the right direction of thought. He caught a furry movement on the side of a tall tree, a boat chugged on the river, smoke rose. He ran down the slope, swerving just in time to avoid a short, uniformed fellow raking leaves onto the asphalt path.

He sprinted toward the playground, his legs working well, but nothing like they had when, as a teenager, he had surpassed his schoolmates in the hundred-yard dash, possessing in his coach's words "the best two legs of the decade," until the surprising day when he had woken up to find his running power strangely altered. Vanished overnight; his fabulous, fabled legs a thing of the past. "I'll be damned," the coach had called out, examining him as he ran. "Your legs are gone." Victor had cast a worried but ultimately reassuring glance down toward the turf. Well, he could still run and he buzzed through the playground gate at a good pace and, slowing down, so as not to be huffing when he found Sonya, he began to look for her. Nowhere. Not in sight. He indulged himself in a leisurely lope around the playground, looking at the women who bent over the sandbox or spread their thighs around seesaws.

The air felt good. He increased his pace as he ran out of the playground; his belly did not joggle. The park worker was still raking, using controlled, energy-saving movements of the arms while his feet stayed in one place.

Why had he never thought of it? He ought to have become a park commissioner, after spending an apprentice's twenty years pruning trees in the open air. No more worry, no more embarrassed lunches with a still-editing Samson. No more imagined cardiac sensations. And Sonya would have pressed his park uniform loyally every weekend until they had saved enough money to send it out for dry cleaning. He slowed down and came to rest a few feet in front of the raker.

"Lots of work this time of year," Victor offered, pleased to appear without an overcoat before this hardy fellow, his cheeks reddened from running.

"Oh, yes," the man kept raking.

"What kind of leaves are these?" Victor asked, scuffing some heavy leaves beneath his feet.

"Ironwood," the fellow said. "Ironwood out here, and over there, an oak. In the playground, linden."

"Oh," Victor said, breathing deeply, enjoying the air.

"Linden, they grind up and make cough medicine. They put them in playgrounds to protect the kids. It's a medicinal tree, healthy."

"Oh," Victor said. The park raker couldn't be more than forty. Maybe thirty-five? Maybe younger. His face was weathered and his hands streaked with dust. His talking, breathing, raking were all one connected piece.

Victor stood by and watched. There seemed an easiness between the men and Victor sensed no imposition in his presence. He took a step closer.

The park attendant pointed to a papery globe the size of a pumpkin lying in a hole where the roots of a tree had been dug out that morning by the mobile forestry unit on its rounds of the city's parks.

"Yellowjackets, wasps," he said, indicating to Victor where he should direct his gaze, but there was little to see.

"Will they sting?" Victor asked, looking over gingerly, drawing back an extended foot.

"Naw," the attendant said. "Dead." With one word he summarized the last weeks of the wasps, which, as the temperature had dropped, very early this year, had first allowed their otherwise well-cared-for furry bodies to become dusty, then dragged the maturing larvae from their cells and thrown them out of the comb to drift toward the bottom of the pit; the about-to-be-abandoned nest must stay clean. Then they had hungrily ripped open the youngest eggs for a final meal before dragging themselves to the exit hole of the nest and slipping over the edge, their light, stiffening bodies floating on the currents of earth-encased air, drifting to rest on the body-strewn floor that awaited them. Only a few fertilized females born the preceding week had survived; stupefied, they lay in the crevices in the bark of nearby trees.

"Dead?" Victor repeated, turning away to look at the slate gray of the river.

"How do you like this job?" Victor resumed, shifting the position of his feet. "Must be nice, working outside all the time. Keeps a man in touch with nature." He jiggled the keys in his pocket.

"Oh, I'm not outside so much as I used to be," the park attendant answered, pausing in his raking and pushing back his hat to talk in earnest. "I'm the foreman here. I got to tell everybody else what to do, I got to keep the place clean, inspect the toilets, paperwork. My laborers are both out today, so I'm raking again. I like raking." He returned to the stroking of the asphalt with the wooden-pronged rake.

"Why don't you rake more then?" Victor answered, annoyed, disappointed in the vision of park foremanship.

"I'm pulling down two hundred and seven dollars a week, and that's cash, in my book. I can't go back to raking at a hundred and eleven. I got kids."

"Oh," Victor said. He was silent thereafter. He moved a step away, so raking didn't even pay enough.

"I was a climber, a pruner," the foreman reminisced. "I could get up a tree faster than any of the other fellows. I scored a hundred points on my climbing test." He looked up to the top of a tall tree nearby. "See that?" he pointed skyward. "I was up there seven years ago, beautiful, that's a beautiful tree. You can see half of Jersey." He turned to relocate his pile of leaves and resumed raking.

Vaguely depressed, Victor ended the conversation and left the foreman, to walk slowly toward Riverside Drive. Maybe he'd be able to see Sonya from the top of the incline.

. . .

By the river, Sonya studied the heavy sky that had
turned the water gray. She was tired of the playground,
of Pauline and her endless complaint from the adjoin-
ing bench; of the teacher on her own bench and her
ceaseless questions; even of Nicole and her answers.
The English professor wouldn't be on the bench today;
it was Friday, the day she taught eighteenth-century
poetry. Sonya was bored by the nurse and irritated by
Supermum, a name given to the pucci-scarfed woman
upon the advent of her third child. Now Supermum
walked with an infant strapped to her chest, pushed a
toddler in the stroller, and held the hand of an older
boy who walked beside her. Supermum discussed bar-
gains in cosmetics and where to go for slimnastics and
how much wheat germ was good for fatigue. Sonya
had sworn off reality for the afternoon.

She went looking for Sonya along the riverbank.
But there was no reflection in the water, the opaque
surface seemed, instead, to draw Sonya in, to absorb
her in the currents. Victor had forgotten to mend the
carriage jump seat and so Peter sat in the carriage
behind Olivia, who, not quite able to sit upright, leaned
against her brother.

The sky did not curve upward into the dome she
remembered from the brittle autumn zeniths in the
sky over her back yard in Eugene, but that had been

the center of the world. She pushed the carriage slowly along the riverside, watching the eyes of her children, whose gazes were seriously turned toward the water. Peter remarked occasionally on boats, their size and speed, and Olivia creased her forehead into an alert and puzzled frown as she tried to fit together the images that lay at some distance in front of her eyes, in a space to which her vision had not yet adjusted and where the separateness of individual objects was questionable.

There had been, in those days in Eugene, no women in the sky. A blue dome rotated, swinging a sun-hole and a moon-hole from horizon to horizon and beyond the dome there was a yellow fire, lasting for-ever, that had been given the name of God, who was a Dad. He had a Son who lived in a slyly shifting cumulus location. Girls in the sky would have been blasphemous. She reached the northern end of the river wall; there were no men fishing so late in the season. She chose the cement bicycle path that led upward to the mall and then ascended through trees to Riverside Drive.

She glanced cautiously among the trees. Was Di-ana just about to branch in or out of the hickory tree? Were the sky guys getting ready for a great convergence in the up-above? Such-a-One would surely attend, promptly and eloquently groomed, carrying a teacup and a saucer in one hand, by the saucer only, her minc-ing steps not allowing her gigantic robe, woven in solid gold by the entire working population of Japan and without a seam, to raise up a wind in the sky. Mummy

Afflictions would be at hand, holy cow, Sonya, you're
not even Catholic! She pushed faster up the hill.

Big Boy would be there, shaking hands, smiling,
using the toilet, doing everything just right, just as he
had been told to do. The Great Babysitter would be as-
suring the adults that they were adults while he took
them by the hand and laid them down to bed, putting
out the light, tiptoeing, and telling lies until the door
clicked shut. Daddy would be there too, or perhaps just
his leg. The gargantuan shoe placed firmly horizontally,
the black silk stocking clinging to the ankle bone, the
herringbone pants hanging over the sock and then, if
you craned your neck way, way back, stretching high
into the zenith, the calf, topped by the knee, the knee
bent, at the apex of power, disconnected from the
horizontal thigh which existed in another plane and remained out of view. What would they do up there?
Fight? Would Mum N sit on Daddy's knee while Such-
a-One went *Tsk tsk* and Mummy Afflictions looked
away? Would Big Boy try to push her off while the
Great Babysitter stared blandly off, preoccupied? It was
anybody's guess. What a crummy bunch! Enough of
them! Where were Hero and Heroine? She pushed out
of the trees onto Riverside Drive and saw Victor clearing the top of the incline. Ah! She belonged somewhere,
she moved toward him. He was like heat, generative.
She was more reflective, a silvered surface.

Victor waved and ran toward Sonya, who was
smiling. He was relieved to see her, to feel the shadow

lift as he encircled her once-more slender hips with his hands. She experienced life on a different wave length from his, a place where she could afford to be fearless of death or decomposition. She probably already saw him as two thirds water, one tenth potassium. He pulled Peter out from behind a slumped and sleeping Olivia and seated the boy on his shoulders. Sonya resettled Olivia and they all waited pedagogically for the light to turn green before crossing.

A young couple on the other side of the street were kissing while the light burned red. At the green, both sets of pedestrians set out toward one another. In the middle of the street, the girl who had been kissing looked up and smiled, entranced at the sight of Victor carrying Peter. The boy, unsmiling, looked away and took his arm from the girl's shoulder.

Maybe

The alarm rang and Sonya silenced it. She made her way quietly to the shower and luxuriated as the warm water ran down her body. Nobody hammered on the bathroom door, screaming "Mummy!" She clasped her hands around her legs just above her knees and did the yoga exercise of sucking in the stomach. She practiced raising her leg from the correct, inner thigh muscle. She turned off the water and dried herself with Victor's big towel. She dressed in the clothes she had hung the preceding night on the back of the bathroom door. Leaving her feet bare, she carried her clogs into the kitchen. After she set coffee on, she opened the front door and picked up *The New York Times*. She even let the emptied wastebasket sit outside the door, nothing right now but indulgence. She sat on a stool and ate breakfast and read a few pages of the *Times*. The baby woke. She recreased the *Times* for Victor, took down a heavy plastic apron to cover the new pants suit, wrapped it around herself, and tiptoed in to pick up the baby. Peter woke up. Victor woke up.

An hour later the babysitter arrived from the baby-sitting agency, another of their plump, middle-aged German women wearing a partially clean nylon uniform and walking bouncily on thick rubber soles. She examined the environs through thick-lensed glasses, frowning at the wicker heads but smiling at the books. "A home of culture," she offered. Sonya nodded. "This is my son," Sonya said, indicating Peter in a wet-bottomed pajama suit. (In whom I am well pleased echoed through her mind, but that was the father's statement.) "This is my baby," she said, handing Olivia in a damp jump suit over into the arms of the nurse. "And my husband is in the bathroom," she said, pointing to the light under the bathroom door.

"Goodbye! Goodbye!" she called a few minutes later, kissing the baby in the warm crease of the neck, stroking Peter on the head, running her hand into the hair on Victor's bare chest. She picked up the Moroccan leather envelope she used for a briefcase and shut the door behind her. She ran down the stairs and flung open the front door. She walked briskly along 80th Street to the subway. Her body seemed to move faster than usual, her spring to be as bouncy as that of the hired nurse. The sensation reminded her of a long hike up Mount Hood when she was a teenager; when they camped for the night, her father had lifted the heavy knapsack from her shoulders and she had seemed to rise up an inch in a reflex action. And now here she was released from the harness of shoulder bag, carriage, and two live bodies. There's a fire engine, she thought to herself, but I don't care! She enjoyed waiting in line for her subway token. She enjoyed the dank smell of the underground. She moved her neck this way and that, feeling her earrings turn. A woman pushed in front of her in the line. A man swore at her for letting the woman get away with it. She was all alone! Alone! Alone! She slipped her token in the slot and was shoved from behind. She was carried, smiling, in a general mass of population into the downtown subway and stood pelvic bone to briefcase with a Prussian-style gentleman whose nose warmed her face with exhalation.

Free. She let her body fall with the lurch of the subway. Leaned far into the briefcase. She studied the advertisements and workaday costumes. The women were getting younger, the men older. She came out into light at 50th Street and decided to walk to the office. Sixth Avenue was as megalithic as she remembered but Fifth more shiny with brass. Madison exuded a smell of paper and Park did not look well, the haze collected in it. Lexington was junky and crowded while Third seemed new, unformed, anonymous.

"Sonya, my dear!" Harold said, swiveling in his chair. "Hey, Charlie, she's here!" He rapped on the glass divider separating his office from that of a small library where photographers hung out and researchers read. Charlie was the best photographer. "Have you had coffee, Sonya?" Harold asked, his gold-rimmed spectacles glinting before his plump face.

"Why, no," she answered. "I'd love a regular."

"Berenice!" Harold stabbed the button on an intercom system. "Bring in a regular."

Sonya felt like falling into the chair by Harold's desk. Berenice arrived and held a paper coffee cup in front of her. Sonya's hand trembled as she accepted it, and she couldn't look Berenice in the eye.

"Hiya," Charlie said, in his fake brusque manner. He didn't look any older. His marvelous hazel eyes connected with hers and Sonya reached out her hand. So this was paid labor! She took her hand away from Charlie's before she really wanted to. Harold handed her folded and gathered sheets on one of the texts. She scanned it for her photographs. There was her own clear photograph of water bubbling in a glass pot, two bubbles perfectly formed beneath the ceiling of air and a third breaking its way out of water. Not a classic like the drop of milk falling into the glass, but nice.

"We're coming up on astronomy," Harold explained. "All picture research of course!" He laughed at his own joke.

"Oh?" Sonya heard herself saying. "What?" she

flipped through the sheets and set them back on the desk.

"How to make a sun-tracker for your windowsill. That kind of stuff." Harold jabbed out a cigarette into an ashtray already littered with butts.

"With a kid in the window, that kind of stuff," Harold reiterated as he swiveled toward her, sipping a coffee. "We figure you're our best bet for locating kids," he said.

"Oh," she replied. "Sure, I can find them all ages." She felt disappointed. Harold had not described the project when she had phoned.

"Here's the list," Harold said, and presented her with a list of six scenes to be shot.

"Looks simple," she said. "Except for the sun-tracking. Got any research on that?" She had almost drained her coffee. She hated how-tos and she'd rather shoot fish than kids.

"Berenice will tell you who's working on it. You can read it here in the library if you want. Trouble is, the deadline's next week. It's a rush job." Harold pursed his lips.

"Oh," she said, wondering how she could fit it in. Well, it was a simple job, really. And it was important she show herself willing to fit into Harold's schedule. "That's okay," she answered, draining the last of the coffee. "Next week." Just to be working was good, that was the plan, wasn't it?

Sonya settled into a chair by a metal file in the

library. She glanced at her watch: eleven ten. She set to work reading on the sun-tracker, a piece of cardboard punched with holes through which the sun shone onto certain but varying spots on the sill according to the time of the solar year. She leafed through surrounding material. Shots of a girl by the same tree on her third and fourth birthdays were captioned with a statement that the child had made one trip around the sun between poses.

She glanced at her watch again, five after twelve! An hour gone by! So much had gone on in her head, in a few inches of gray matter, while hardly anything had happened with her muscles—her fingers had turned a few pages, her eyelids had blinked, and she had crossed her ankles once.

She was due back at twelve thirty, having engaged the sitter for the exact four-hour minimum demanded. She raced through the rest of the research and refiled the folder; she said goodbye to Berenice, and to Harold, but she couldn't find Charlie. She dashed out to the corridor. Twelve thirty-five, already late! She'd have to take a cab.

She leaned back against the seat of the cab. She'd have to spend several hours at night on the project and that would make Victor mad. Here I am, commuting, she thought, exhilarated; the cab cut across Central Park, leafless as on her first trip to New York. Time had brought her onward from that trip, was bringing her out of her exhaustion. Where next? Who next? Anyway, she should work toward a regular arrangement with Harold by experimenting and perhaps she shouldn't tell Victor about her plans before they were clinched. He might count on the money, she might feel pushed. How were the children? She hadn't thought about them. Had they eaten? When would she eat? Sonya trusted the baby-sitting agency. But still. She paid the cab driver hurriedly and rushed up the apartment stairs and fumbled with the door. She heard Peter's voice coming from the kitchen. Her heartbeat slowed down.

She worked on her project Friday evening and planned to get up early to continue work on Saturday, her morning off. When she woke, she found herself looking at Victor's sleeping face, his bushy hair, his forehead. It must have been a year since she had looked at the corners of his closed eyes from such close range.

"Hey," he said at breakfast. "Why don't we all picnic today?" He leaned out the open kitchen window to test the temperature. "The last of the outdoor days!" He brought his upper half back into the room. "I'll get up tomorrow, too, and take care of the kids, you can work then." Although Victor was capable of having forgotten his promise by Sunday morning, she decided to risk it.

"Okay!" she said, "Okay!"

An hour later they were out on Riverside Drive near the site of the sewer construction. They were a two-carriage family now; Victor stopped the stroller to zip up Peter's jacket while Sonya waited behind the pram that was buffeted by a strong wind.

"Men working overtime," Victor said, watching the crew. They took a brand-new cement path around the site, looking north up to the view of apartment houses on a slight bluff over the park.

"That's where the estates must have been," said Victor, indicating the higher apartment buildings. "Rich chicks in billowy dresses looking out over their lawns to the edge of the cliff and then over the river to Jersey, drinking gin fizzes."

Sonya looked up at the bluff, imagining the nurse-maids who spent hours on summer afternoons preventing children from tumbling over the rocks. They turned westward, toward a tunnel which would bring them to a path that angled above the train tracks and finally down to the river.

"This whole park used to be an extra back yard for the rich," Victor said, remembering the dizzying micro-film he'd projected at too fast a pace, checking on out-dated human interest in the park. "When people visited New York, they'd hire a carriage or bike and wheel along the drive to look out over the trees toward the far west and think about the Pacific, Oregon, baby, your hangout."

They pushed their carriages under the tunnel, listening to the echo of their ooohs and imagining the reverberation of the fuuuck youuuuouuu that was scrawled in large chalky letters on the inner wall of the tunnel. As they covered the slope upward toward the traffic circle, the wind increased and they drew their necks into their collars. On the sidewalk atop the circle, Peter struggled to get out and see the train tracks below and Victor held him up to the grating of a window which opened onto a huge space falling to the tracks sunk deep in the darkness. Sooty air whistled in the dungeon-like space.

Peter wiggled down and they rounded the traffic circle and dropped their carriage wheels slowly down the flight of marble steps to the fountain below. "The train's coming!" screamed Peter. They paused in the middle of the stairs to turn their faces toward the crenelated stone wall behind which the train roared as it tunneled forward, then they slowly resumed lowering carriage wheels down the steps. Sonya imagined the riverbank giving way to train tracks and the tracks being covered by the city at a slow-motion pace, the laying of the mall, the planting of trees, probably at a formal ceremony, their taking hold on the landscape, and flourishing while the rich folks on the bluff degenerated into middle class and slowly admixed with the poor. She and Victor had sat among the poor before they were married, on a Fourth of July as they watched green fireworks burst and arch and fall into the river where they were silenced with a *pfft*. The poor had pressed sleepy children to their shoulders and Sonya had longed for a child to say oooh at the arcs of the burning flashes.

No water was spouting in the fountain; the basin was dry and littered with a pair of last summer's socks. Wind blew through the arches that framed their passage to the balcony above the boat basin. The light on the river shone clear. It was cold, the boats looked abandoned to the winter. Sonya could no longer see her own playground, it was out of sight over her right shoulder. That part of Riverside Park which was of her time and history would soon be recorded on maps filed at the Museum of the City of New York, yellowing into something out of Ur. The children in the season of Peter and Alexandra who had learned to walk along the benches, the women whose words and abjurations had not spun off into air but been implanted in the forgotten children, would one day be unearthed as rusted stroller handlebars or misshapen silver bracelets by the trenchers of future sewer betterment.

They walked and wheeled to an unfamiliar playground close to the river. It was deserted. Victor lifted Peter from the jump seat and Sonya parked the carriage in the sun, carefully positioning it so that Olivia's brows would cast their narrow shadow on her delicate, closed eyelids, protecting her eyes from the sun's rays and leaving the rest of her face in its warmth.

Peter took Sonya's and Victor's hands and swung between them, their three shadows fell on the ground in front of them, reproducing exactly the dotted pattern that Sonya had read about somewhere—the very pattern that shortwave stations were sending off into space to the listening antennae on distant planets, a pattern which was meant to indicate that the inhabitants of the sending planet reproduced sexually. A kind of opener, as it were, a prize little bit of info for the far skies, and something which might appear either refreshingly quaint or reassuringly familiar—who could tell?— should it ever be received. As yet, there was no indication that the electrical impulses, sent out in sequential, linear order, had been snatched up and realigned in a two-dimensional plane to form the proper picture, pointillistic in the extreme.

They separated near the slide. Alone, Sonya felt her leg muscles tensing to move her feet toward the slide. It was not her brain giving direction to her feet, as her gym instructor had warned against, but the reach of ankles and toes that was bringing her to the base of the slide. Then, slowly, she was climbing. For two years she had foregone sliding but now, with no one watching, why not? From the top she could hear distant traffic and the voices of Victor and Peter by the jungle gym and, for a second, the wind against old newspapers by a low wall. She pushed off and it was faster than she expected; she stood, barely in time to avoid landing on her giant, brittle backbone.

A high whistle pierced the air.

"Must be noon!" Victor called. "Let's eat!"

"That's the blasting," she explained, walking toward the jungle gym. "First that high whistle then in a few seconds, the blast." She glanced at the carriage.

"Big noise," Peter warned, his hands against his ears. Victor climbed quickly to the top of the gym.

The ground shook, a muffled blast followed. Peter tensed, Olivia gave a little cry. Victor climbed down. "Couldn't see a thing," he reported.

"Creepy, isn't it? The blast?" Sonya said in a low voice to Victor. "Sometimes the children in the playground scream together, after the explosion."

He put his arm around her. "It's nice to be alone," he said. "Even in the city." They walked toward the parked carriage. "Let's try to decide about moving out this weekend, once and for all. You tell me when you're sure what you think."

Sonya felt loosed, floating, unsure. She tried leaving it to the muscles but nothing happened in her ankles, nothing in her toes. She did not answer Victor, but her brain directed her to place her hands on the handlebars of the pram and she pushed. "Let's eat!" she said, motioning to Peter.

On a park bench by the river wall, Sonya unpacked the hard-boiled eggs and cut them with the handle of a spoon. The wind blew bits of crumbled yolk into the baby's hair and over her handknitted blanket as she lay drinking from her first propped-up bottle. It blew against a paper cup full of apple juice that Sonya transferred to the safe hold between her knees. Victor pared an apple with a sharp knife.

"Last time I peeled anything outdoors it was a cucumber with my brother's bayonet in a field outside

Skibbereen." Victor peeled casually, stuffing apple peel into the empty bread wrapper. "I saw a bull climb up on a cow and I wished him happiness and a son." He cut off a slice of apple and handed it to Peter.

Siding with bulls. Sonya smiled. A man of style, she had always admired him for that. And I, Olivia, have wished for you. She unwrapped a third egg; it was perfect, oval. She unwrapped a fourth, dented, broken in at one end. Her fingers were stiffening as she started to hand the perfect egg to Victor. No. She juggled the eggs and handed him the one with the dent. She bit into the perfect egg. Soon it would be time for gloves, mittens. She remembered a pair of green mittens she had owned as a child, with white stripes running around the wrists. The snow crusted on them and she sucked the water and snow from them when her mother wasn't looking.

She refilled Victor's coffee cup and handed it to him, across the lap of Peter, who was stuffing Swiss cheese into his mouth. She patted Olivia. The coffee was warm. She warmed her fingers between her thighs. She watched the light on the river; it was brittle, the sky looked hard, painted on enamel by Fra Angelico. Her school yard in Oregon had overlooked a dammed river. The wind blew over the water. Soon it would be time for Halloween. Knees reddened by the wind, she had run home to see her mother. Her mother took the sharp knife and cut eyes in a pumpkin, nose and mouth. The yellow light shone out of the holes of the orange sphere. "It is yours," her mother said later, setting it in the darkened windowsill of her cold upstairs bedroom. Her mother's permanented hair was curly and her slim body was silhouetted by the light from the jack-o'-lantern as she bent over the sill. Then she came to the bed where Sonya lay, wrapped in a warmed flannel sheet and heaped over with quilts. Sonya put her hand out and her mother held it as she sat in a rocker beside the bed and leaned her head back, shutting her eyes before she sang. Sonya remembered with surprise how much she had once loved her mother.

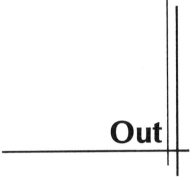

Out

Sonya packed her photographic stuff separately. She chose the grocery box still possessing flaps so that she would be able to bend them down one after another, and so cover the box when it was full. Carefully, she set the box on the floor of the kitchen and bent down its flaps. She stared into the empty box.

"I want to live the life I sing about in my song." She heard the sound of Mahalia Jackson singing in the living room. Sonya had been playing that record the first night Victor had rung the doorbell to her apartment, long before he had a key of his own. Mahalia Jackson, another age. The past, boxed, stretched over with soft plastic. Abruptly, the music stopped.

"Hey Sonya!" Victor called from the living room.

"Could you bring me my pliers?" He must be dismantling the hi fi.

Sonya searched in the tool drawer. Let him find them himself! "Hey!" she called back lightly, "I can't find them!" She walked out of the kitchen to gather up her camera stuff from its scattered locations. She heard Victor rummaging in the tool drawer. He was humming the tune from the Jackson record but there was no more sound from the hi fi.

She picked her Nikon out of the top drawer of the bureau and wrapped it in a few pages of the *Times* lying on the bed. She fetched the Yashica with its long lens from the bottom drawer in Victor's desk and opened another fold of the newspaper.

"Hey, Sonya?" Victor came to the doorway of the bedroom. "Looks like we'll be up all night, want a pizza? I'll go out to the corner."

"Great," she said. She turned the long lens in his direction. It flattened his face against the wall of the hallway, several feet behind where he stood.

Hello. Hello. He mouthed the greeting to her silently, with only slightly exaggerated movements of the lips. His upper lip was like their son's, with an infinity sign exactly in the middle.

Sonya. He mouthed her name. Her mother had named her after Sonja Henie, a doer.

"Maybe you'll photograph more in the new place," he said, putting on his heavy jacket. "Mushroom?" he asked. "Sausage?"

"Half of each," she answered. "How about you?" She wrapped the long lens in newspaper. She hadn't used it since November when she had finished the sun-tracking assignment. Harold had explained then that the sun-tracker was the last loose end in the science series. He could not give her any work until spring, when he began on social studies.

She walked Victor to the door and after he had gone lined the bottom of the carton with paper. She placed the camera and lens on top of the paper and then went into the bathroom for the chemicals and developing box. The box was chipped on the corner. It wasn't light-safe any more. When had that happened? She threw it in the wastebasket. She examined the bottles of chemicals on the windowsill. One held only an inch of liquid; she threw that out, too. She tightened the cap of the other and wrapped it in an under layer of Kleenex, walked into the bedroom for more newspaper, and then into the kitchen, where she suddenly unscrewed the cap and poured the contents down the drain. She tossed the still-wrapped bottle into the wastebasket. If she planned to make the best of the move, she might as well begin with basics. She would buy a completely new stock of chemicals next week. There was a pantry off the new kitchen with a door that could be shut to make a darkroom. She had already measured the counter with her eye, it was wide enough to hold the enlarger; maybe she would have to build it out a little more with a shelf. She could toilet train Olivia early and use the diaper money for film. Or they could eat cheap cuts of meat. Why wait for Harold, she could start in with studies of snow, of the wind. Unpacking must not take top priority.

Victor came back with the pizza. "Here," he said, handing her the pizza and a small paper bag. She set out the pizza on plates and opened the paper bag, expecting cheese or the capers, which only Victor liked. It was a roll of Plus-X.

Olivia, the egg-bearer, had thousands of eggs lying in her miniature ovaries. All she had to do was smell sweet and show a little deference to males and some of those eggs would be fertilized, the gene banks of half of Europe drawn upon. The thousands of throwaways slipping and sliding over pond bottoms would, in Olivia, be avoided. Accuracy was so high with the sperm-thrower inserted into the very body of the egg carrier that Olivia herself would take unnatural steps to limit the number of fertilizations to two or three. She and her sperm-maker, who had begun at puberty to produce millions and millions of sperm, would together protect the two or three young and see that they reached the reproductive phase before Olivia and her mate slipped into the detachment of body elements that foreshadowed extinction. Olivia, sitting in her carriage, watched the bare trees and smiled while Sonya pushed her.

Sonya and Victor had packed till three A.M., and although she was tired Sonya wanted to make sure the children got to the playground before the trip. If they ran around now, they'd be less restless in the car. Besides, she wanted to go to the playground one last time, herself. When her parents had sold their dining table, she had set her alarm for two a.m. and crept downstairs in the night to say goodbye to it. She pushed the carriage with one hand and watched Olivia closely—she could see her daughter much better now that her son no longer straddled the carriage in his special seat. Him she pulled behind her, using a trike fork that hooked around the handles of his Christmas tricycle. At the top of the incline, she shifted weight, as the tricycle moved rapidly ahead and she used the fork to restrain its progress down the hill. They passed Pauline's son, walking alone up the incline. He was wearing a peajacket and dungarees, no more nylon snowsuits. Although he couldn't be more than four, he had the face of a person; he was grown. His mother and sister lagged yards behind him. Would the children of Pauline's son be brought to play here? Probably not.

Sonya's grandchildren would never see this playground either. Nor would her own children visit it after today. She wished she could give them this circle of linden trees as their history, replete with the lost toys of her own childhood, the China doll with the red cheeks and too-white skin pressed into the crotch of one tree, the red yarn doll of her mother's caught in the branch of another. But Sonya had only her own generation of history here. Her grandmother had skirted New York and rolled westward from Maine, her pale English face shining from the hub of wagon wheels that turned across Iowa and Nebraska. Had she settled on New York's West Side, her grandmother might have sunk gradually beneath the pavement with Sonya's mother and Sonya and Olivia, in turn, rising up to replace her in the baby park. But what did it matter, the hundreds of miles by wheel from ocean to ocean? The real journey was temporal, from minute to minute, through season to season, new life brewed in old RNA molecules, old and new life somehow linked together by fission and fusion, a trick of numbers. Clever. Invisible.

Peter's trike crept ahead of her and got going too fast. Both vehicles were in front of her now and Sonya restrained each with a different pressure. The snow was crusted brightly between the rails of the iron fence that bordered the incline and, trite though the image was, Sonya wished she'd brought her camera. She blinked as she hurried behind the two vehicles, trusting to her memory cells to keep the sight for her, the power of the memory cells lasted only seven years but there were so many cells—the snow's whiteness was probably already coded into hundreds of knots of gray matter, and its shine was about to be scattered to thousands of widely and safely distributed bundles, while its granularity waited to be matched with the brain's granularity of bunched proteins. The trike and the carriage began to slow into the bottom of the incline and then ceased rolling. Sonya unhooked the fork and Peter pedaled himself through the gate of the playground.

Sonya resumed pushing the carriage and made her way into the playground. Seating was chaotic on Sunday afternoons. There were no familiar faces on her accustomed bench. No Nicole. No English professor. Not a single Jonathan or Alexandra. She sat down between two Sunday fathers whose children she knew by sight but not by name. She picked up Olivia and settled her with pebbles and a cup near the bench.

It was not her park any longer. Dawn after the lover's last phone call. The knowledge of her departure had already cut her off from the park. The women on nearby benches looked smaller. She had begun to forget their particularities as she might forget those of a Mandan tribe who had snatched her from her parents' village and whose ways and manners she had quickly memorized as essential to survival. Now she was going away, had indeed begun her journey. Peter headed toward the trike jamboree in the center of the playground. He rode caboose on a string of three-year-olds, their legs pumping up and down, moving the wheels of their machines forward across the asphalt. Years this side of initiation, the peer boys pedaled or pummeled in a great arc, safely within the vision of the women who encircled them.

The slide offered its inclined plane, the jungle gym its ultimate in right angles, but the playground was indifferent to Sonya. She saw the playground without herself in it, empty space, blue-painted bench between the two men, her body vanished. By the bench an abandoned Olivia crawled unguarded with last summer's crop of babies, dampening the knees of their snowsuits, squealing and passively allowing the older children to take their toys away. Energy-storing fat had begun to collect around their jowls and above their knees. Now they depended mostly upon their chubbiness for the irresistible appeal that kept them looked after, especially since they had begun to drool bits of obnoxious moisture. The newborns of the winter, set in carriages in the wan January sun, infants with scrawny necks and thighs, still smelled sweet beneath their layers of wool and canvas.

Life pumped slowly, buzzed almost inaudibly about in the playground, the women running toward menopause, the babies trapped in their buntings, the wings of the birds flapping sporadically and desperately, the slowed sap in the linden trees, the eddying into heat around the thermoses of coffee, friction fought all the way down the slide. The inanimate metal fence would outlast them all. First the women, and then the children would be replaced, then perhaps some chains in the swings, a tree, bricks in the comfort station, then might come a shift in the chemical content of the air causing the blue benches to be entirely vacated. Sonya's fingers were freezing. She picked up Olivia and collected the sand bucket and the thermos cup and packed her belongings in the outdoor bag and swung the fork around Peter's trike and they were off out of the playground and up the slope.

"Today's the day," Victor said, grabbing Sonya around the waist when he led them into the hallway. While they were out, he had wrenched a built-in bookcase from the children's room of Aunt Monica's now twice-abandoned apartment and pushed a few last things into cartons and barrels. Monica's spindly furniture, which had long ago been swamped by the wicker heads, and by the door tables and beds, as well as by the baby paraphernalia that had littered the apartment, was now liberated and collected in the farthest corner of the living room. Narrow aisles ran through the debris and over these Sonya skittered, preparing lunch, changing diapers, and looking for lost combs and brushes.

"I'm doing it!" Victor assured them all, striding into the kitchen in his jeans and fur-lined boots. "I'm taking care of you. You'll have to pay attention when we get there," he added with mock sternness, reaching into the refrigerator. "Peter, you'll handle twigs for firewood, and Sonya, you'll do roots and berries." He swung himself up onto a seat on the kitchen counter, drinking directly from the milk carton.

"The fire's out!" Peter replied. "EEEEEEEEEEEH!" making the noise of a siren as he quoted from his fire engine record.

"I won't go for food tonight," Victor explained. "I'll probably have a hell of a time twirling the two little sticks together."

"I can wrap up a few things in plastic bags," Sonya volunteered. "I suppose I'll be busy from the time we get there weaving a cradle for Livi." She sponged down the counter, standing close along Victor's thigh to reach behind him. She picked up the *Times* to throw it out.

"Hey, wait a minute." Victor interrupted her action and grabbed the paper. "This may be our last touch with the written word." He opened the real estate section. "Just checking," he explained.

Peter picked up another section of the paper and held it in front of his eyes. "P begins with Peter," he reported from behind the newsprint. "M begins with Mummy," he waved the paper in the air. "D begins with Daddy!" He threw the paper at Olivia's feet, which dangled out of the highchair. She laughed; she enjoyed attention of any kind.

Sonya dismantled the kitchen bulletin board. She could throw out the note to remind her to tend to the diaper man, she had already forgotten and he would come tomorrow and find nothing. She had sent off the check to the gym instructor. Harold's phone number she knew by heart. The picture of Peter in his first snowsuit. It did not look like him any more. She slipped it into her apron pocket. The recipe for chicken with lemons, she had tacked it up on a hot summer night. The doorbell rang.

When the movers came in, Victor vanished to shave. The big items reachable from the paths through the furniture went out first and then the babies' cribs, Victor's skis, and Sonya's enlarger. There was time for Sonya to shower while Victor, to cut labor costs, helped the movers carry things down the stairs. Finally, they could see the floor, the hallway where they had first met, the place where the amniotic fluid from the sack where Peter had spent his first nine months had seeped, the still-polished floor beneath the couch where Olivia had been conceived, the painted slats in the children's bedroom that had been Sonya's photographic studio, and before that, Monica's music room. The rooms were empty now, the curtains had been taken down and folded. They did not even know who would take over the fantastic lease, thirty-three years old, as old as Sonya. It was like bones, this floor, the last view of the bones of the dead old maid.

"Okay, family, single file," Victor commanded, raising Peter to his shoulders and starting downstairs. Sonya picked up Olivia and the plastic bag full of extra paper diapers and a bit of food and followed him down the stairs, leaving the door open for the movers to take a last few boxes. The weather was freezing. Sonya could see Victor's breath condensing as he walked down the steps of the brownstone to the street. The trees at the end of the street were ice-glazed and sparkling and the river was a cold gray-blue. Sonya shivered and drew her coat around the baby.

"This is nothing, nothing compared to the far north I'm taking you to, the pastures, the ice-capped mountains." Victor warmed up the new car and slapped his hands together.

"I'll need a buffalo coat right off!" Sonya shouted over the sound of the motor and the crunch of the door that shut with an unpleasantly metallic sound as she settled herself and Olivia in the back seat. Victor eased the car out of its tight parking place. She was leaving behind the place where her children had been born.

"No more population explosion, no more parallel parking," he called over his shoulder, addressing himself to the empty mid-afternoon street. They drove toward Broadway, Sonya turned her head to look over her shoulder out the back window, straining to see the trees by the foot of the street where Monica and she had walked, separately. Victor made a left onto Broadway and she faced frontwards as they drove out to the parkway.

If it was hard to leave 80th Street, it was easy to be separated from her possessions. They were all neatly combined in the hold of the moving van. It would not matter if the van should move off the Saw Mill Parkway, vanishing down a wrong lane, unprogrammed, circuiting out like a lost satellite to become part of traffic that never ended. The four of them were the essentials, mov-

ing at different rates away from conception, falling outward from the weakening pull of fusion into the world.
The real world, her father had always said, meaning,
oddly, other people. The real world, she had testily
replied, is stones. It no longer mattered which of them
was right.

To keep the children from being carsick, they rode
with the windows open and their coats buttoned,
scarves wrapped around their necks. It was not a long
drive to Chappaqua. Sonya leaned her head back, but
kept her eyes open, looking up out of the window, the
way she had ridden as a child. She saw clouds, cuttings
in what had once been hills. She heard the blinker for
the highway turn-off, she saw the tops of trees along
suburban streets, she heard the sound of the tires
pulling off concrete onto gravel.

"Last stop!" Victor called, turning the key in the
ignition, raising the bar of Peter's car seat. Sonya sat
up and looked out the open window at the three-story
Victorian house. The afternoon light was soft, but it did
not blur the precision with which the shadows of the
porch railings fell against the white walls. "Women and
children first!" Victor lifted Peter out of his car seat
and set him on his feet on the driveway in front of the
car. Victor's boots made a reassuring sound in the
pebbles as he came back to open Sonya's door. He
steadied her with an arm as she gathered Olivia close
and stepped out of the car onto a frozen front yard.

A Note on the Type

This book was set in a typeface called PRIMER, designed by Rudolph Ruzicka for the Mergenthaler Linotype Company and first made available in 1949. Primer, a modified modern face based on Century broadface, has the virtue of great legibility and was designed especially for today's methods of composition and printing.

Primer is Ruzicka's third typeface. In 1940 he designed Fairfield, and in 1947 Fairfield Medium, both for the Mergenthaler Linotype Company.

Typography and binding design by Christine Aulicino. Composed, printed, and bound by The Haddon Craftsmen, Inc., Scranton, Pa.